# Shattered Faith
## Rebecca May Hope

Gabriel's Horn Press
2019

Contact editors@gabrielshornpress.com

Published in Minneapolis, Minnesota by Gabriel's Horn
Press

Publisher's Note: This novel is a work of fiction.
Names, characters, places, and incidents are either products
of the author's imagination or used fictitiously. Apart from
historical figures, all characters are fictional, and any
similarity to people living or dead is purely coincidental.

First printing: October 1, 2019
Printed in the United States.

For sales, please visit www.gabrielshornpress.com

ISBN-13: 978-1-938990-49-6

To Lois and Günter,
whose words and example inspired me
to cross the finish line,
or, as they would say, to "close the loop."

# Table of Contents

# Acknowledgments

The first chapter of *Shattered Faith* originally appeared in the Summer 2017 issue of *Sixfold* Magazine as a short story, "Coyotes from Kazakhstan." Two irritations, one minor and one major, converged to inspire that story. At my daughter's slumber party, her friends woke me in the middle of the night, insisting they'd seen coyotes prowling our yard and approaching our front door. The next day I learned that my bank accounts had been closed because someone from Kazakhstan had attempted to hack them—about the time the "coyotes" had supposedly visited my home. And so a story idea was dropped into my lap, which turned into "Coyotes from Kazakhstan" a decade later. Not wanting to leave Faith in the predicament she was in at the end of the story, I eventually wrote a happy ending for her.

The character Jen is an amalgamation of dozens of talented and precious homeschooling moms I encountered over my twenty-seven years of homeschooling. Through her I pay homage to the many wonderful women who inspired me and enriched my children's lives. Günter Hofmann assisted me by checking the German phrases in Chapter 3. Lucas Brist designed the cover. My writers' group, Night Writers, gave me invaluable feedback that improved the manuscript.

Being involved with American Christian Fiction Writers (ACFW) has also benefited me as a writer. I thank their contest judges, who reviewed my work as volunteers. *Shattered Faith* won first place in the ACFW First Impressions Contest and was a finalist in the novella category for the Genesis Award.

Finally, I thank those who supported and encouraged me throughout this process: my faithful first readers, Connie and Joey; my publisher, Laura Vosika; and my family.

# Chapter 1: Coyotes from Kazakhstan

Faith shot up in bed, her heart pounding. Lance rolled onto his side, moaned, and plastered his pillow over his head. He had a meeting in the morning. Since she was the work-at-home spouse, it was her duty to make sure Isme's slumber party didn't get too rowdy.

"I'll find out what's going on."

Faith stumbled to the chaise lounge for her robe and poked her feet into her slippers. She tiptoed out the door and swung it closed. Still groggy, she gripped the handrail as motion-activated stairway lights illuminated her descent. In the family room, lights blazed on a babbling huddle of six ten-year-old girls wearing PJs.

Faith squinted against the glare. "Isme?"

"Mommy!"

Arms encircled her waist.

"Coyotes! There's coyotes out there!"

Stroking Isme's back, Faith felt perspiration through the silky pajama top. The crazed, wide-eyed faces of the girls turned toward her.

"Don't worry, girls. It's no big deal." To reassure them, she made eye contact with each one. "They're far away, back in the preserve." The spooky wail sounded scary, but the creatures rarely approached humans. Isme knew that and should have calmed her friends. "They howl back there a lot in summer, don't they, Isme?"

Isme stepped back and raised her hazel eyes. She tightened her lips in a determined line and shook her head with three defiant turns of her neck, making her brown hair flap against her cheeks. "We saw them. Two of them. We saw the coyotes stand."

"Where?"

Isme pointed toward the far wall of the room, made up entirely of windows, floor to ceiling. The glass reflected back the line of girls as they all turned, arm in arm, then pointed in unison like a wonder of animatronics. The blinds, tight accordions eight feet above the floor, were almost never lowered. This side of the house backed up to the nature preserve that bordered Purgatory Creek as it wound its way toward the Minnesota River. Situated at the end of a five-hundred-foot drive in an area of executive homes, their house was not exactly isolated, but it was private.

"Let me see."

Faith switched off the light. The girls shrieked.

Faith eyed the stairs, hoping Lance was sound

asleep by now. "Shush!" A couple of whimpers answered. Great. The girls would tell their moms she'd yelled at them. "Isme's daddy is trying to sleep. It's very late."

She cupped her hands around her eyes, resting her nose against the glass. Only the eerily yellow full moon and a dim security lamp lit the edge of the pool. But any movement out there would activate the lights beside the patio doors below.

Isme positioned herself at Faith's side and mimicked her stance. "They're gone now, Mom. But they were right there." She pointed to the north side of the swimming pool. "That's where we saw the coyotes *stand.*"

"You didn't see them move?"

"Yes, we did. They kind of crept along by the pool fence." Hunching her shoulders, she rotated her arms to simulate the skulking animals. "And then they both stood, like this."

She straightened to her full four-and-a-half feet and curled her hands like a dog begging for a treat. Faith squinted at her daughter in the faint light that filtered in from the hallway. Could she be serious? It wasn't like Isme to prank. She must have given in to the other girls.

Rolling her eyes, Faith let out an exasperated sigh. "Isme. That's enough."

The devastation on the child's face stabbed Faith to the core. Isme never lied.

"They did, Mom." Isme sniffed. "Really!"

Faith squatted and held out her arms. The

teary-eyed girl flew into them.

"Isme, honey, coyotes don't stand on their back legs. I don't know what you saw, but it wasn't that. Okay? Maybe you saw a reflection or something."

Forcefully Isme pulled away, her lips drawn tight again. She posed like a begging dog. "They were just like this. Everyone saw them." She raised her voice. "You guys! Didn't you see the coyotes stand—like this?"

One by one the girls held up their paws. Faith clenched her teeth. She couldn't resolve this now, but Isme—and perhaps the girls' mothers—would hear more about this tomorrow. She checked her watch: 2:15. No, today. But after they'd gotten some sleep.

"Okay, well, no harm done. They're not there now. Everyone into your sleeping bags." She shooed them forward, forcing a playful smile. "Last one in is a rotten egg!"

The girls, stifling giggles, scampered into their sleeping bags. Faith pulled Isme's up to her chin and kissed her on the cheek. She turned her face away. Great. Lance was sure to be on her case about the noisy sleepover, and now her daughter was upset with her.

* * *

Faith waved goodbye as the last of the girls, draped in a beach towel and dripping from one last morning dip, boarded her mother's minivan. She sent her own little girl to bed for a nap—sans protest. She could use one herself, but her prime writing hours were slipping away. Hopefully the whole summer wouldn't be like this. Even when Isme was at school, working from home was full of interruptions. And lately it didn't take much to distract her.

In her office, she ignored the words of the obstinate half-finished novel on the screen. No use trying to focus on it until she figured out how to handle the coyote incident. Coyotes standing hadn't been the end of it. An hour later she'd jolted awake again. More screaming. Isme claimed one coyote came back. She saw it sneak under the deck and heard it scratch against the patio door.

"It scratched five times. One, two, three, four, five." At each number she made a vicious, curling grasp with her right hand. "We were so lucky it didn't get in, Mom."

The three girls who were still awake—two had fallen asleep—claimed they heard the scratching, too. Faith checked to make sure the walkout was secure and then calmed the girls, sleepiness smothering her anger. But thirty minutes later she was back in the family room, rocking Isme and her best friend, Maddie. They insisted they saw the coyote slinking away from the house, dragging its rear leg as if injured. By that time the girls were delirious, worn out from imagined terrors. Maddie fell asleep on Faith's shoulder while Isme dozed on her lap. Finally Faith extricated herself and crept back into bed. A few hours later Lance, in an awful mood, barely growled two words before leaving for work.

While the other girls were in the pool, Faith pulled Maddie aside. Maddie admitted the girls hadn't seen or heard anything at first, but when Isme seemed so convinced, they played along. Eventually they started believing it. But in the morning light, no one remembered actually seeing or hearing anything. They might have. But they weren't sure.

Isme never made up tales. Having been raised in Sunday School, she took her lessons seriously. But she clung fiercely to these stories. Faith sighed. She'd sit her down for a long talk when she woke up from her nap—before her father came home. Best not to get Lance involved. Now that he'd made partner, his law practice was more stressful than ever.

Faith rolled her shoulders and neck, cracked her knuckles, and typed a few words. The phone rang. Of course.

"Faith? Good!" Brian, their personal banker, sounded relieved. "I caught you."

They couldn't be overdrawn. She kept plenty in the reserve line. "What's the problem?"

"We had some major hacking last night." His voice was low and confidential. "I've closed all your accounts."

"Seriously?" More distractions. It would take

hours to update all their auto-pays. "Do you know what a hassle that is?"

"I know, I know. I'm really sorry. But this was a big one, and the fraud department thinks they've got the goods on the guy this time. He's been planting Trojans for years, stealing identities. Goes by the moniker Lucky12345. They traced him to Kazakhstan."

"Coyotes stand."

The automatic murmur escaped Faith's lips. She crossed from her desk to the window and gazed toward the pool as a surreal sensation prickled her shoulders.

"What? No, Kazakhstan. It's by Russia."

"Yes. Yes, I know where it is." Faith blinked hard and jiggled her head, trying to shake away the odd feeling. "Tell me what I need to do." Brian's answer barely registered. She scanned the tree line beyond their property. "Do you know when—what time—our account was hacked?"

"Mmmm. Hold on." Keys clicked on Brian's keyboard. "I've got the report up. This is an internal page—I'm not supposed to share it with clients. So don't spread it around. Okay, got it. The first attempt was 2:04 a.m. CDT. Next one: 3:10. Those were unsuccessful, and he got away. And the one we nabbed him on—that was 3:42. Crazy, huh?"

"Yeah, crazy."

Faith disconnected, plopped down at her desk, and dropped her head into her hands. Her brain buzzed. A nefarious creature, begging outside. Scratching at the door, *one-two-three-four-five. Lucky* he didn't get in. Slinking away, wounded. Kazakhstan … coyotes stand.

It was too odd. Isme had seen coyotes simultaneously with the hacking attempts—all three times. Faith rubbed her neck and forehead. She needed sleep.

* * *

That night after dinner Faith joined Lance in the den. He flipped off his computer monitor when she entered. Good. Lately he'd been better about that. She hated it when he kept eyeing the screen while she talked.

Wearing ancient jean shorts and a ratty T-shirt, he looked as attractive as he did in his business suit. His deep brown eyes under ridiculously heavy eyebrows, his dark spiked hair, and the tinge of five o'clock shadow along his jaw gave him a somewhat swarthy, mysterious appearance. Always irresistible. Two years ago she'd have rounded the desk, wheeled back his chair, and plopped herself onto his lap. But that was no longer their pattern.

Instead she sank into the green plaid arm chair. She poured out the story of Isme's fantastic visions that coincided perfectly with the hacking.

"Yeah, yeah." He seemed distracted. "That's good. I like it."

"You *like* it? Our accounts were hacked, and

our daughter sensed it somehow."

"Best idea you've had since *The Graveyard Whistler.*"

That was her first successful crime thriller. Three years ago now. "It's not a novel synopsis." She glared. "It really happened. To us. Last night —I mean, this morning."

"Huh. Is Brian on it?"

"Of course." She ran her fingers through her hair and drove her nails into her palms. He wasn't tracking. "But what do you think it *means?* How could Isme have known?"

"It means you got a story idea dropped in your lap." He kept glancing at his darkened monitor, bouncing his knee almost imperceptibly. "I'd run with it."

She bit her lip. This was going nowhere. "You think it's just a coincidence."

He was probably right. What else could it be?

\* \* \*

"Could be the Universe trying to send you a message."

If anyone could shed light on this weirdness, it would be Collette, collector of all things kooky. They sat in a corner booth eating lunch at Collette's favorite organic place.

"That was Monday, right?"

Dressed in a peasant dress and flip-flops, Collette didn't look like someone who lived in a two-million-dollar mansion on Lake Minnetonka. Her husband, Steve, had made partner a couple of years before Lance, but Collette was as casual as if she were still backpacking across Europe and living in hostels.

"The night of the 'honey moon.' Hmm. That night was the first time in seventy years we've had a full moon on the summer solstice."

"Sure. Whatever." Raising her shoulders, Faith squinted across the table. "But why would the Universe send me a message through my daughter? My banker has a phone."

Collette fingered the crystals on her funky necklace, custom designed to balance her moods and magnetic field. Her red hair fell in waves onto her shoulders, and her freckled face had that third-trimester glow. As she closed her eyes in concentration, her pretty rounded belly rose and fell hypnotically under the swirling paisleys of her sundress.

Collette opened her eyes slowly. "You're thinking too small. Think bigger, outside the box. Not about Isme, but about the hacking."

"Nothing mysterious there." Coaxing a cucumber slice into the dressing, Faith wondered if contacting Collette had been a smart choice after all. She tended to read too much into things and was hardcore New Age. "Hacking happens all the time."

"Yes, but Isme's vision augurs the real meaning." Collette's spooky bicolored cat eyes, with their central golden circles rimmed by blue, bore into Faith. "That your greatest treasure is in jeopardy."

Faith's heart skipped. "I know. I'm really worried about her."

Collette squeezed her eyes shut for a moment, then laid her fork across the arugula. "How are things between you and Lance?"

The seemingly irrelevant question didn't surprise Faith. As a hobby, Collette ushered her friends toward nirvana by recommending workouts, supplements, meditation, or whatever. She fancied herself a life coach who never charged a fee.

"He's stressed out, as usual. More cases than he can handle. But that's a good problem to have, he always says. Who knew there were so many crummy products out there, right?"

"That's why they brought Katrina on." Collette held a jicama stick between her fingers like a cigarette. She nipped off a bit. "Have you met her?"

"Katrina who?"

Collette's eyes scolded. "Katrina Williams. The new junior counsel."

"Lance tries not to bore me with office stuff." Faith faltered under Collette's skeptical stare. "Well—I think he doesn't want me putting his office into my novels. You know."

"She's a knockout. Striking. Long black hair, blue eyes, great figure." Collette finished off the jicama. "If Steve wasn't so crazy about me, I'd be worried."

Faith dropped her eyes. The arugula, limp with vinaigrette, was easier to confront than Collette's intense gaze. Was she probing for the details of her and Lance's love life?

That would be a bland story.

"Lance prefers blondes." Armed with a good angle, Faith looked up. "Every girl he ever dated was blonde."

Collette's dangling earrings, etched with some sort of Celtic symbol, waved doubtfully as she rocked her head from side to side.

Faith squirmed. She had to get this conversation back on track. "So you think Isme is psychic?"

Collette speared a cherry tomato. "Maria could find out. She could put her under the pendant."

Maria, Collette's energy consultant, kept Collette, Steve, and the boys supplied with every conceivable nutritional product. Collette's supplement pantry, centrally located in her designer kitchen, was legendary.

Faith swigged down the last of her bitter green tea. She needed something more credible than a swinging crystal. She needed a real answer.

\* \* \*

"Mass hysteria. Not a doubt in my mind. Google it."

Lance's mother suggested the search during a phone conversation after Faith filled her in on the sleepover. As the former precinct coordinator for Al Gore's presidential campaign, Wanda felt she'd assisted with inventing the Internet, so she did her part to keep it afloat.

It wasn't a bad idea, so Faith complied. Google instantly delivered 231,000 results for *Mass Hallucinations* and 19,900,000 results for *Group Hysteria.*

"Lots of strange stuff can be explained that way." Wanda's keyboard clattered in the background. As usual, she had her phone on speaker. "Not just the Salem Witch Trials. Those don't even make the top ten. Find the top ten list and check out number two. It just shows how fragile men's egos are. Lance's too, you know. Gotta keep stroking them all the time."

Faith already regretted sharing her concerns. She wouldn't reveal the attempted hacking. As soon as she could get a word in, she'd steer the conversation back to Isme's ballet lessons.

"Those other girls are as much to blame as Isme—probably more. Tell their mothers that."

"They've never mentioned it."

"Good." Wanda's voice reverberated. "We can't let Isme's social standing suffer."

Faith scowled at the phone. Isme had *social standing* now? "I'm sure her friends just thought it was a fun slumber party game."

Wanda, like Lance, worried too much about

pleasing the right people, as if their fall from grace might be as meteoric as their rise. Not that long ago Faith and Lance had lived in a two-bedroom apartment while she supported him through law school on her teacher's salary.

Faith scrolled through the "10 Most Bizarre" post. A year-long laughter epidemic in Tanzania in 1962. Textile workers who became ill from supposed June bug bites. Four hundred people who danced themselves to death in France in 1518. Nothing remotely similar to Isme's experience. There it was, Wanda's favorite—something to do with men's egos. Number Two: Thousands of men in Singapore who feared their private parts were shrinking. Faith shuddered to think what search terms Wanda had entered to find that page that she seemed to know so well.

After Faith disconnected, she kept googling. She found a *Psychology Today* article about a woman who called 911 to report that eight men were slicing the roof off her car. Doctors found nothing wrong with the woman, but four people who touched her, including two policemen, started hallucinating. The woman's opioid patches might have been to blame.

Had Isme been influenced by opium? Horrified at the thought, Faith hurried to the family room and began searching the entertainment center for mysterious powdery residue. With every drawer she opened, she felt more foolish. That Lance could be using drugs was as ludicrous as his having an affair.

"Whatcha lookin' for?"

At Isme's voice, Faith jumped and slammed a drawer shut. "Nothing, sweetheart."

"Can we bake Daddy his favorite cookies?"

Tan, lean, and bright-eyed, Isme looked perfectly healthy. On the outside, anyway.

\* \* \*

"Faith? Gretchen here." The pediatrician's voice was crisp yet concerned. "The nurse gave me a note saying you had a quick question. I have just a minute before my next patient."

Normally Faith wouldn't risk straining her relationship with the woman who was a friend as well as Isme's doctor, but she was worried enough to break her own rules. She shut the door to her office in case Isme came back inside.

"What does it mean when kids start lying? And won't admit they are?"

"Isme's lying?" Gretchen sounded surprised. "About what?"

Suddenly Faith realized she was about to ruin her daughter's reputation. "No—uh—I'm asking for a friend. One of Isme's friends."

"Of course." Gretchen's voice dripped irony. "Tell 'your friend' it's called *pseudologia fantastica* or *mythomania*. In adults it's an attention-seeking behavior, but in kids it can be a form of compensation." Her tone softened. "Is everything okay between you and Lance?"

Faith's pulse quickened. Why would Gretchen take the conversation there? "Sure. Fine." Her conscience stabbed. She was a feeble liar for someone whose career was fiction. "What's the treatment for pseudo-whatever?"

"I'll get you the name of the children's psychiatrist we refer to. She's great. I know things haven't been easy for you guys. A stillbirth is traumatic for the whole family—children and fathers, too. Especially after you tried for so long. Even though it's been a year now, Isme might be— oh, they're signaling me. The front desk can give you that name. Call me at home tonight, and we'll talk more."

Faith stared at the silent phone. She still wanted to ask what it meant when the lies the child told turned out to be true, but in a nonliteral way, but the child didn't know that, and the child still wouldn't admit to lying. But that might prompt a referral to the adult psychiatrist.

\* \* \*

"Of course you're not crazy." Jen wrapped her arm around Faith's shoulders and squeezed. "Just a concerned mom."

Soaking up the sunshine, they sat together on a bench at the playground. Jen had texted—as she had so many times over the past year—and this time Faith took her up on her offer to meet at the park. Jen's five kids and Isme were playing tag on the maze of tunnels, bridges, and slides.

Faith relaxed, easily settling into their old friendship. "But isn't it odd?"

"I think it's awesome." Jen jumped up, ready to run toward her youngest, who had just taken a tumble, but her oldest was already there, brushing off the little one and making her laugh. Jen sat again, pulled off her glasses, and polished them on her shirt. Putting them back on, she angled herself toward Faith. "It's more common than you think. They're like living parables. Real-life incidents that have spiritual meanings. Symbolic meanings."

"That's a thing?"

"Oh, sure. God often speaks in symbols. The Bible's full of them, right?"

Jen should know. She majored in Bible and music at the Christian college where she, Faith, and Lance had first met. Now her career was marriage ministry, motherhood, and homeschooling her brood.

"Okay, but what's the point?" Faith sucked hard on the straw of her water bottle—as if enlightenment lurked at the bottom of the Nalgene. "What does it mean?"

"Foreshadowing. Sometimes a warning." Jen tapped her fingers together in front of her chest as if to some internal melody. "Or maybe just to let you know: God is protecting you. The coyotes never entered, and the hackers didn't steal. Because God has your back."

Had Jen just composed a praise and worship song on the spot?

Faith hadn't paid much attention to God lately. It didn't feel like He was watching out for them. "About the parenting class—sorry we dropped out. Lance has been so busy—Sunday mornings are one of the few times we can spend together."

That's what they told each other when they'd stopped going to church—but mostly Lance slept in on Sundays or played golf.

"I'm glad you're prioritizing your marriage." Jen nodded toward the playground. "Look at them! So cute!"

The six sweaty children sat in a ring, shaded by a platform, playing a boisterous clapping game.

"By the way—do you want to go to the marriage retreat? Registration's closed, but I could probably still get you in. It's next weekend."

*Prioritizing your marriage.* Didn't that take two? Lance wouldn't be caught dead at a marriage retreat. "Oh, sorry! That's Lance's annual convention. He'll be out of town."

Faith shifted uncomfortably. Somehow that truth felt like a lie.

Jen shrugged. "Maybe you can make it to the next one."

Seeing Isme give Jen's youngest a hug, Faith's heartstrings quivered. She would have made a wonderful big sister.

"Do you think Isme could be psychic?"

"I wouldn't use that word." Jen studied Isme

as she sifted pebbles through her fingers onto the giggling toddler's toes. "But some people are especially sensitive spiritually. That's good, because they can be more in tune with God. But they also can be targeted by the enemy or tempted to use their third eye on their own. You can pray and ask God to close it."

A third eye? Faith didn't relish that diagnosis for her daughter.

* * *

The third eye could be developed, evidently. Clairvoyant children, according to the websites Faith found, had an open chakra that, without deliberate training, would naturally close as they grew older.

The sooner the better. Those sites about children and ESP creeped her out. Ads for psychics kept popping up—offering to teach your child the ropes. Not a chance! This one incident had already consumed her for three weeks. Isme never talked about it, but Faith had spent hours upon hours researching and getting advice, trying to make sense of it. Hours she should have spent writing.

But who was she kidding? Her writing career was an ego booster only. Just one of Lance's product liability cases brought in more income than she could earn from ten years of teaching—or twenty of writing. But without her career, she'd have nothing—except Isme.

She closed all the open tabs and maximized her novel. Before she typed a full sentence, her sister's ringtone interrupted. She wanted them to join an impromptu family reunion at Wisconsin Dells. Would Lance be okay with that?

Faith brought it up during dinner.

"Can't get away." He put up his hand to decline the green beans Faith passed him. "I'm already gone the end of that week for the convention."

"Aw, Daddy!" Isme flashed a pleading pout. "It's a water park!"

"You and Mommy can still go."

They'd be gone four days and get back a few hours before Lance flew out for his trip. Isme was thrilled. Faith needed a break. No coyotes, no hackers, no visions.

\* \* \*

The vacation worked. Faith resolved to not mention coyotes, and they almost vanished from her mind. On the four-hour drive home, she figured out how to turn her languishing novel into a trilogy of novellas—complete with a child psychic. Why not? Lance would be happy she'd taken his suggestion. She couldn't wait to run the idea by her agent.

After helping them unpack the car, Lance set his own suitcase at the front door and pulled Faith into his arms. Rubbing the sweet spot in her lower back, he kissed her—a long, lingering kiss. Tingles rippled through her body—more tingles than she'd felt for the last year—and she pressed into him.

She nuzzled his earlobe and whispered, "Wish I was going with you."

After one more luscious kiss, he pulled away. "Too late now. Flights are booked. I'll see you Monday."

He brushed his hand under her chin the way he used to in the early days.

She watched him stride down the sidewalk, stop to twirl Isme around, and hop into his Lexus. Her heart swelled. They *were* a happy family.

As she started a load of laundry, she imagined Lance's return. A candlelight dinner. Sensuous classical music on the iPod building to *Bolero* after Isme had gone to bed. Humming, she plopped a few last items into the tub, dipped into the laundry powder, and rhythmically sprinkled the load. Just when she crashed the washer lid shut, vocalizing *Bolero's* crescendo, Isme's voice resounded from the hallway.

"I'm biking over to Maddie's!"

Energized by the ever-quickening beat as Bolero replayed in her head, Faith unpacked the cooler in record time, then headed toward her office to call her agent. At the foyer, she stopped in her tracks, shaking her head. Isme, in her excitement to see her best friend, had left the front door wide open. Faith closed it and reset the alarm. She retrieved her cell phone and, leaning back in her office recliner, tapped her agent's number.

Her agent loved the novella trilogy idea. Just as Faith disconnected, three short beeps sounded from the front door, and Isme's feet pattered upstairs. Maddie must not have been home. Excited to tackle the rewrite, Faith positioned herself at her desk and powered up her computer.

"Mom!" Isme appeared in the doorway, a look of wild surprise lighting her face. She beckoned with her arm. "Come quick! There's a cat on your bed!"

Faith rose. "A cat?" Possibly a stray had wandered in through the open door. "That gray and white one that's been hanging around?"

"No, Mom." Isme shivered with delight. "It's all black—with blue eyes."

Faith steadied herself against her desk. A sick feeling washed over her. "Isme, black cats can't have blue eyes."

She had discovered that while doing research for *The Graveyard Whistler.*

"This one does. They're the same color as the pillow case and sheets. It's laying with all the rumpled sheets piled up around it—like it's Queen Cleopatra or something. You'll see!"

Isme ran down the hall and bounded up the stairs, two at a time. Faith trailed behind, her stomach burning. There were no blue sheets for their bed.

Entering the master bedroom, Isme blinked hard. "It's gone."

The bed was made. Faith felt her skin crawl as dread descended.

Isme teared up. "It was laying right there!"

"Lying."

"I am not!" Isme clenched her fists at her side.

The teacher in Faith had spoken by rote even as her mind swirled. "It's *lying*—not *laying*. 'It was *lying* right there.'"

Isme's hands unclenched, and fear spread across her face. "Who made the bed?" she quaked.

Faith folded her daughter into a hug. She was sweating. "Go drink some water, hon. You need to hydrate."

As Isme padded down the steps, Faith inched toward the bed, her heart pounding. She slid the layers of decorative pillows aside—for once Lance had arranged them perfectly. She braced herself before turning down the silky mauve comforter. Sweat popped up along her hairline and under her arms. Slowly she drew back the cover to expose a blue pillowcase. She gasped, lunged for the pillow, and heaved it across the room. It came to rest against the leg of the chaise lounge, the single long black hair still sticking tenaciously in place.

# Chapter 2: Angel from Eden Wood

Faith shuffled over to the chaise lounge, dropped to her knees, and buried her head in her arms against the mauve upholstery. She had been so stupid. Everyone had tried to warn her— Collette, Gretchen, Wanda—they had all sensed the brewing affair somehow. Jen had tried to get her to prioritize her marriage. Naively she had whistled past the graveyard, ignoring their hints and her own nagging doubts about her relationship with Lance.

How could he? He had vowed to love and cherish her, to keep himself only for her. Until death. That was a promise he'd made before God and a church full of people. Only eleven years ago. Who was this man? Either she didn't know Lance as well as she thought she knew him, or he had changed. The glamour of success had seduced him away from his vows. Or Katrina had.

Of course, the hair had to be Katrina's. Faith didn't know anyone with long black hair. Turning toward the bed, she envisioned the seductress lying amid rumpled blue sheets. Her stomach flipped violently, and she ran toward the master bath. Kneeling in front of the toilet, she tried to heave up the specter of Lance with another woman, but nothing came out.

"Mom, are you okay?"

Isme stood in the bathroom doorway, looking queasy herself.

Faith jumped to her feet. "I'm fine, honey." Seeing Isme's scowl, she quickly crossed the ceramic floor. "Actually, my stomach doesn't feel so great." She placed her hand on the girl's shoulder. "How about you?"

Tears pooled in Isme's eyes. "Now that you mention it, mine feels gross, too. Do you think we ate something bad? Is that why I thought I saw a cat?"

"Maybe." Faith quickly ushered her past the chaise lounge and the blue pillow and into the hall. Her heart thumped wildly, but she couldn't let Isme catch even a glimpse of her fury. She had to protect her. She forced a smile. "Maddie wasn't home?"

"She's at the dentist." Once outside the master bedroom, Isme's face relaxed. "Her sister said she'd send her over when she gets home."

"Maybe you should lie down in your room before she comes. I'll bring you a can of ginger ale."

Faith smiled at Isme as she pulled the door

shut, then scowled. She stomped down the steps, pounding her fist into her palm to help satisfy the urge to strangle Lance. She started for her cellphone but remembered the ginger ale. Pulling it from the refrigerator, she barely refrained from crushing it in her grip.

With Isme settled on her bed with a book, Faith felt her nausea rising again and ran for her own ginger ale. She wouldn't call Lance yet. She had to think. Reluctantly she returned to her room. She shut the door, strode to her nightstand, and snatched a mauve envelope from the drawer. Steeling herself, she picked up the black strand of hair and deposited it inside, then licked the envelope shut. With the back of her hand she wiped the taste of betrayal from her tongue.

She picked up the pillow she'd thrown across the room and pelted it against the chaise lounge over and over again. *This is for you, Lance. Take that, Katrina! For doing it in my bed. For breaking vows. For spurning me.*

As the chaise lounge took its beating with infuriating stoicism, her rage only grew. At last she drop kicked the pillow toward the door, then slumped onto the lounge. She took a slow sip of ginger ale, then squeezed her fists tight and forced herself to think.

As much as she wanted to call Lance right now and scream in his ear enough to melt his cellphone, she couldn't risk Isme overhearing. And once Isme was in bed for the night, Lance would be at the gala. The one time during his trip that his phone would be turned off.

On the other hand, there would be something luscious about confronting him in person. The second he walked through the door Monday night, she'd dangle the hair in front of his nose and demand an explanation. She snorted. There would be no *Bolero* after all.

Instead, they would engage in an epic battle— the first of their marriage. She and Lance seldom argued—they were so compatible. Unless he had only pretended to sync with her and was leading a double life. How long and in how many other ways had he deceived her over the years? Who was he when she wasn't around?

Gingerly she grasped the blue pillow between her thumb and forefinger and returned it to the bed. Shaking the taint off her hand, she glared at the enigmatic blue sheets. In novels and movies, the tell-tale signs of a husband cheating on his wife were things like lipstick on a wine glass, a woman's cigarette left in an ash tray, or the wife's toiletries rearranged in the bathroom. Lance didn't drink or smoke, so no use looking for the first two. She returned to the master bath. All her lotions, sprays, and soaps were exactly where she'd left them before she went to Wisconsin Dells. Only one used towel from this morning hung on the hook, and only one towel and Lance's underwear and pajamas were in the hamper.

What about the mauve sheets that should have

been on their bed? Where were those? She hadn't seen them in the laundry room, but they could be in the dryer. She made her way downstairs and checked the machine, but it was empty. She stepped into the garage and checked the dumpster. Nothing. Yesterday was garbage pickup.

Why would Lance buy new sheets? She didn't want to think about that. But blue? Leave it to Lance to pick the totally wrong color. He was clueless when it came to decorating. He couldn't even arrange the pillows— Of course. Katrina, not Lance, had stacked the decorative pillows on the bed so perfectly. Faith sipped frantically on the ginger ale, then took a deep breath.

Perhaps Katrina had put the blue sheets on the bed. But why? Was it proper etiquette to bring one's own sheets when seducing another woman's husband? Was Katrina rubbing Faith's face in this, exulting in victory by mocking her? She felt the urge to scratch Kat's eyes out.

She searched the linen closet with such vigor that Isme heard and called from her room. "Do you need help, Mom?"

"No. It's okay."

The mauve sheets were nowhere to be found.

* * *

Faith flipped off Isme's light and closed her door. She had forced herself to watch *Zootopia* with Isme and Maddie, but her mind was racing the whole time. She hadn't felt like cooking, so she'd ordered pizza. Not a good idea. It burned her stomach even now.

With Isme in bed, she could continue snooping. What other clues of Lance's escapades during her absence lurked around the house? Thankfully Lance hadn't called—she couldn't talk to him without shouting, and she had to hide this from Isme for as long as she could. At tonight's gala dinner, he'd be busy schmoozing with the other attorneys until late.

Including Katrina. They were staying in the same hotel. He was probably with her right now. She pictured the raven-haired beauty she'd never seen in a slinky black evening gown.

Faith wandered into Lance's office. Everything looked in order—his stack of legal journals and photocopied articles lay in their normal jumble atop his desk. She sat down at his computer and turned it on. She had never considered investigating his online behaviors, but suddenly she questioned everything. Why after all these years would he start turning his monitor off when she entered the room? Naively she had thought he was becoming more considerate, but it could be just the opposite.

Hands shaking and teeth chattering, she maneuvered the mouse to pull up his browsing history. Her stomach dropped. There was no history. Well, just one day. Yesterday. So he was routinely deleting his history, but must have forgotten to do so yesterday.

Most of yesterday's links seemed tame enough —the news websites he checked every day, investment sites, and legal blogs. Suddenly her blood froze in her veins. Several URLs in a row seemed sketchy. She opened one and quickly closed it. Porn. Soft porn? Hard porn? She had no idea—she'd never expected Lance to ogle trash like that. Disgusted and sickened, she shut the machine down. Her face burned with shame. What had her husband turned into—and when?

She pushed herself out of the chair and bolted from the room, slamming the door behind her. In her own office at the other end of the house, she sank into the recliner. Her heart pounded, and her lungs refused to take in oxygen. Lights flickered before her eyes. Dropping her head between her knees, she stared at the speckled cut Berber carpet just inches from her nose. Slowly the room stopped spinning, and she gradually straightened.

She had to talk to someone. But who? Her mother and sister thought the world of Lance—she couldn't bear to hear their shocked reactions. Jen would understand. She and her husband mentored plenty of messed-up couples through their ministry at church.

Unfortunately Jen was at the marriage retreat this weekend. Still, maybe she could talk for a few minutes. Calling this late might be rude—it was eleven o'clock—but the thought of trying to sleep with this crisis raging caused her chest to constrict again. She picked up the house phone and keyed in Jen's cellphone number.

Tim answered.

Faith plastered on a fake smile. "So sorry to call so late, Tim." Her voice came out squeaky and quivering. "Can I talk to Jen?"

"Sure. I'll get her."

From the tone of his voice, her cheery pretense hadn't convinced him.

In a moment she heard Jen coming to the phone. "Faith? Are you okay?"

The dam burst. Tears streamed down Faith's cheeks and she could hardly get a word out. "Not really."

"I'll be right there."

Faith hugged the silent phone to her chest.

\* \* \*

Wringing her hands while she paced the entryway, Faith focused only on the fact that help would be here soon. At the sight of Jen coming up the walk, she opened the door, her finger to her mouth. She didn't want to wake Isme.

In the dimly lit kitchen they prepared their tea in silence, then climbed onto the stools at the center island.

"Thanks for coming." Faith bit her lower lip. "I didn't expect you to leave your retreat."

"Camp Eden Wood's just ten minutes from here." Jen shrugged. "And we've got several other couples assisting this year—so it's no big deal. What's going on?"

Faith gulped. "Lance is..." Her chin trembled uncontrollably, and her eyes stung. "Lance is cheating on me."

Behind her brown tortoise shell glasses, Jen's brown eyes softened. She stood and wrapped her arms around Faith.

Faith sobbed onto her shoulder—the same shoulder on which she'd shed tears of joy the night Lance proposed. Jen had been there at the very beginning of Faith's marriage, and now she was here ... tonight.

Faith pulled away and reached for a tissue. "I just figured it out today." She wiped her eyes and face. "When we got back from our trip."

Jen perched on the stool again, facing Faith, and tilted her head to hear more.

Faith poured out the story, from Lance's sweet goodbye kiss to Isme's vision of a blue-eyed black cat to the discovery of the long black hair on their bed and the blue sheets.

"I'm sorry, Faith." Jen adjusted her glasses thoughtfully. "That sounds bad—but it doesn't prove he's having an affair."

Faith scoffed as she bobbed her tea bag up and down in the steaming cup. "It's all the proof I need."

"You don't want to jump to conclusions." Jen pursed her lips. "There could be some other explanation."

With her elbow on the counter, Faith buried her forehead in her palm. "He's been looking at porn online."

"Mmm." Jen sipped her tea. "How long has that been going on?"

"I have no idea. I only checked his history today—I've always trusted him before. Everything was deleted except yesterday's." Faith faced her friend. "But he's been turning his monitor off for months now when I come into the room."

"Okay, that's something you'll need to confront him on." Jen squared her shoulders. "You'd be surprised how common that is, even for Christian guys. But it still doesn't prove an affair."

Faith rolled her eyes. "You're making me be a lawyer."

"Or a super sleuth, like Stacy in *The Graveyard Whistler*."

Faith sighed and leaned against the back of the barstool. "I can do that." She steepled her fingers in front of her chest. "He must have started looking at porn months ago."

Jen nodded her encouragement.

"Yeah, our love life hasn't been great since the baby died."

Jen patted Faith's shoulder. "I understand. Go on. You're doing fine."

"They hired this junior counsel a while back—Katrina Williams. I haven't met her, but I hear she's knockout gorgeous. Long black hair."

Jen scrunched her nose with disgust, but

motioned for Faith to continue.

"Remember Isme's vision of the coyotes?"

"Sure," Jen said. "And the hacking."

"I didn't get it at the time. I was so obsessed with what it meant for Isme." Faith waved her finger at Jen. "But you said it might be a living parable, which I didn't quite understand. But now I do, I think."

"What do you think it means?"

"It *was* a warning, like you said." Faith shivered. "God was trying to tell me my marriage was being hacked. Well, maybe not successfully that time—because the hackers didn't get our money. But this second vision of Isme's shows that the hacking was successful." She ran her fingers through her hair, scraping her scalp with her nails. "The thief got in and stole my husband in my very own bed."

Swirling her tea bag around in her mug, Jen pondered the idea. "That's one interpretation. But it may not be the only one." She squinted at Faith. "What about the blue sheets? That's so odd."

"I'm not sure." Faith shook her head. "I can't find the mauve set anywhere. But I can almost guarantee that Katrina made the bed, not Lance. He couldn't arrange those pillows right if his life depended on it. But they were perfect—just the way I do it."

Jen drummed her fingers on the granite counter top. "Okay, but even then, that just means she slept in the bed, not necessarily with Lance."

"We have two guest rooms." Faith glared. "If for some reason Lance invited her to stay overnight, he'd have put her up in one of those, not in our room."

"I get that." Jen exhaled slowly. "But you've still only got circumstantial evidence. Nothing that you can convict a man on."

Faith scanned the cabinets in front of her. Something had been irritating her ever since she'd sat down. "Just a minute." She stood and pulled a stool toward the refrigerator. "This cupboard's not quite shut. It's driving me crazy." Standing on the stool, she steadied herself against the refrigerator as she reached toward the cabinet above. "I'm becoming OCD in my old age."

"Becoming?" Jen laughed. "I was your roommate for two years, remember?"

Faith turned to roll her eyes at Jen, but suddenly a peculiar tightness nagged her gut. Instead of tapping the cabinet closed, she opened the door wide. As she drew back with a gasp, the stool swiveled under her feet.

Jen flew to the stool and steadied it as Faith regained her footing.

Faith reached into the cupboard. "Here, grab this."

Jen accepted the wine bottle into her hands. She set the bottle on the counter, and Faith passed two goblets down to her. Faith felt all the color drain from her cheeks as her body went numb. She sat on the stool, then hopped to the floor.

She crossed to the counter and picked up the nearly empty bottle in both hands. Tilting it, she read the label. "Truly Irresistible Chablis."

Jen studied her face. "I take it you didn't know this was up there?"

Faith clunked the bottle onto the granite and pushed it away, stretching her arm full length. "You know we don't drink."

Jen nodded. "Wasn't Lance's dad the head of his AA chapter when we were in college?" Jen set the glasses down. "I remember him telling about his dad's recovery."

"That's why Lance always swears he'll never touch a drop. It was horrible at home for him when his dad was drinking." Faith took Jen's hands in hers and stared into her eyes. "Jen, what's happened to him? He's not the man I thought I knew."

"Let's not panic." Jen squeezed Faith's hands and let them drop. She rested a hand on Faith's back. "Let's go to your office, and we'll strategize. And pray. We'll come up with a plan—to make your marriage stronger than ever."

*Don't panic.* Faith repeated the words to herself as she picked up first one glass, then the other.

Jen arched her brows. "What are you looking for?"

"Lipstick."

* * *

Jen settled into Faith's office chair, pulled a writing pad toward her, and selected one of the purple gel pens from the pencil holder. Faith leaned forward in the recliner. Praying together had stopped her heart from pounding, but jumbled emotions—fear, anger, sorrow, shame, and guilt—kept vying for position, muddling her brain.

Sitting straight in her chair, ready to take charge, Jen nodded at the black computer monitor. "Have you stalked her yet?"

Faith flashed both palms in front of her face, closed her eyes, and shuddered. "Are you kidding me?"

Jen shrugged. "Know your enemy." She reached her finger toward the computer's power button. "May I?"

At Faith's nod, she pressed it.

"You're quoting Sun Tzu now?" Faith cringed at the familiar start-up tones, dreading what she was about to see. "What happened to the Apostle Paul?"

Jen snickered. "All's fair…" She clicked a few keys. "*Facebook* or *Linked In*?"

Faith rose and leaned over Jen's shoulder. "*Facebook* first."

When a page of Katrina Williams suggestions came up, Jen immediately clicked on the first one. Across the top of the screen spread a photo of an attractive woman in front of a picturesque fountain backed by a pillared building.

Jen drew back. "Whoa! Is that her?"

At the sight of the raven-haired beauty, Faith dug her nails into the back of Jen's chair. Parted at the side, Katrina's black hair flowed in loose waves well below her shoulder blades as she posed in partial profile, displaying her curves and long, shapely legs. Despite her professional attire, her pose revealed she knew how to make the most of her charms. The square inset showing her close-up revealed piercing blue eyes, high cheek bones, and thick red Angelina Jolie lips above a delicate chin. It could be a glamour shot.

Jen cleared her throat. "Almost no info here. She's not giving anything away. Do you want to send a friend request?"

Faith slapped her shoulder. "Check out her *Linked In* profile."

The same face shot, in a round border this time, popped up. "University of Chicago Law School *summa cum laude*," Jen read. "Princeton undergrad, also *summa*. Long list of professional memberships, some awards, published articles, one previous firm. She's smart."

Faith punched the computer's off button. "Smart and sexy." She flung herself back into the recliner. "I might as well throw in the towel."

"Don't be silly." Jen waved her hand dismissively. "She's not Lance's type."

Faith kneaded her scalp. Maybe he preferred a different type now. Very different.

Jen picked up the pen and hovered it over the

notebook. "When does Lance get back?"

"Monday. Around six."

She wrote one word at the top of the page, another in the middle, and one toward the bottom. She went back and underlined each word with a decisive stroke. "That gives you two days to investigate, and one day to plan your difficult conversation."

Faith's jaw fell open, and she stiffened. "Three days? Are you kidding? I'm calling him tomorrow about this—as soon as Isme's out of the house."

Jen pantomimed a cower. "Okay, okay!" She rolled the chair away from the desk and closer to Faith. "You sure can. That's one way to handle this. But probably not the best way."

"I can't wait three more days to get an answer. Why would I put myself through that?"

"I understand, Faith, really I do," Jen soothed. "But the truth is, time is your ally here—if you use it right. Think about it. If he admits to you over the phone that he's having an affair —which is highly unlikely—you're not going to end that conversation on a positive note. You can't get started on a plan for reconciliation until he's back in town and you can hash things out face to face. But let's say he doesn't admit anything—that he has an explanation for the hair and the sheets. Which is about ninety-nine percent likely. Will you believe him? Lying over the phone is much easier than lying in person, and it'll be much harder for you to read him. So you'll spend the weekend wondering anyway."

Faith nodded slowly. Maybe Jen was right. After all, she was trained in marriage ministry, and she'd counseled many betrayed spouses. "Okay. I promise I won't confront him over the phone."

Jen smiled and shrugged. "You don't have to promise me. It's your decision."

Faith blew out a long breath. "I know. But if I promise you, I'll stick with it."

"Good. In the meantime, you can do more spying." Jen scooted the chair back to the desk and tapped the notebook with the pen. "Who do you know that can shed more light on what's been going on?"

Remembering her lunch with Collette, Faith put her hands to her forehead and drew them down over her eyes and cheeks. "One of the partner's wives—Collette—tried to warn me a month ago. She's the one who told me about Katrina—and how beautiful she is."

Jen set the pen down and leaned forward. "What did she tell you?"

"Just that if Steve wasn't so in love with her, she'd be worried about Katrina herself."  Faith blinked back tears, and her throat constricted. "Meaning that Lance doesn't love me anymore."

"I'm sure that's not what she meant to say," Jen comforted. "Do you think she has any more to tell you? Could you see her tomorrow?"

Faith stood and walked to the bookcase. She straightened the volumes on the top shelf so their spines were even. "Steve's at the conference, too, so she'll probably be available. I could call her in the morning."

The pen glided along the paper. Jen prompted, "Anyone else?"

"Wanda, maybe."

"Lance's mom?"

"She said something kind of odd after the coyote thing." Faith moved to the desk and surveyed the To Do list Jen was preparing. She tapped under the heading *Sunday.* "Put her down there. She's taking Isme on their annual mini-golf outing at the Sculpture Garden tomorrow and keeping her overnight. She'll bring her home Sunday afternoon."

Jen penned *Wanda* under *Sunday*. "What did she say?"

Faith plopped into the recliner again. "She was hinting that Lance's ego needs stroking. Well, that or something else."

Jen cocked her head.

"She wanted me to look up some list of mass hallucinations." Faith rolled her eyes. "She pointed me toward the one where hundreds of men thought their privates were shrinking."

Jen laughed. "Really?"

Faith shrugged. "Wanda can be a bit crass sometimes." She smirked and wiggled her head. "My mom would faint at some of the things Wanda spews out."

"What do you think she was getting at?"

Faith studied her hands in her lap. "I just blew it off at the time, but I suppose she meant that his fertility problem could be hurting his self-esteem."

Jen squinted. "Do you think Lance confides in her about that kind of thing?"

"She could have wheedled something out of him." Faith stroked the microfiber arm of the recliner. "I wouldn't put it past her."

"Okay. So you'll get Wanda alone on Sunday afternoon and pump her for info." Jen leaned back in her chair. "You'll have to get Isme out of the way."

"She'll probably be ready for a break from Nana," Faith laughed.

"That's two possible sources of intel." Jen clicked the pen a few times, then set it down when Faith glared at it. "Anyone else?"

"Gretchen was the other one who seemed worried for my marriage."

"Gretchen Ekblad?" Jen leaned forward again, eyes wide. "What did Dr. Gretchen say?"

Faith felt her face redden. She'd been so foolish. "I called her about Isme's lying. About the coyotes." Embarrassed, she averted her gaze from Jen, who would certainly disapprove. "But right away she asked me how Lance and I were doing. Like she'd had some hints from Lance."

"Lance sees her? Isn't she a pediatrician?"

"She's been our GP for years. Since we know her from church, we go to her for routine stuff."

Jen nodded. "When did he see her last?"

"A few months ago, maybe. For some follow-up blood work."

With her finger to her chin, Jen swiveled in the seat. "With HIPPA regs, she can't tell you much."

"She invited me to call her at home, but I never did." Remembering their conversation, Faith curled her hair around her ear and tugged it thoughtfully. "Maybe she has a way to tell me something without violating any rules. You know that old ruse—'tell your friend I said such-and-such.'"

Jen laughed. "Way too obvious! Wink-wink!"

Faith flushed again. "I'll call her in the morning, too. Maybe she can meet me. Write her down under Saturday."

Jen complied. "I'm jotting a few more things down for you to check—signs of infidelity. Notes or cards in his desk or suit coat pockets, numbers you don't recognize on the cellphone detail, any little gifts that have suddenly appeared. You can check for all that on Saturday when Isme's gone." She finished writing, then stood, looking at her watch. "Speaking of Saturday, it already is. You need to get some sleep."

She offered a hand to Faith and pulled her up out of the chair. "I won't be at church Sunday, but you can call or text anytime. Come over Monday, and we'll plan out your conversation with Lance." She bent over the desk and wrote *Jen* under *Monday*. "Isme can play with the kids. Come around noon, and we'll have lunch." She placed her hand on Faith's back and steered her out of the room, flicking off the light after them. "Until then, keep calm. Trust God."

At the foot of the stairs, Faith crumpled onto the bottom step with a shudder. "I can't sleep in our bed knowing *she* was in it."

Gently Jen raised her to her feet. "I'll help you get settled in the guest room."

After trudging up the stairs, Faith ducked into her closet for her nightgown and robe. Forget washing her face. She grabbed her toothbrush and scurried past the bed, where Jen stood examining the blue sheets.

"Do you want me to take them off for you?"

"No!" Faith yanked Jen into the hallway. "That's a crime scene! They'll stay on until Lance can explain why they're there."

"Gotcha, Ms. Super Sleuth!" Jen laughed as she reached to open the door of the next bedroom.

Gently Faith placed her hand over Jen's where it rested on the doorknob. "Not there. That's the baby's room."

Jen's shoulders fell, her brown eyes softening. "You said you were making it into a guest room again. That was months ago."

Faith didn't bother wiping away the tear that trickled down. She swung the door open and switched on the light, then motioned for Jen to enter. The blue room was just the way it had been a year ago, ready to welcome their new son. She and

Isme had been so excited that they'd set it up months ahead of the due date—but the baby had never come home from the hospital. A red baby blanket dotted with footballs, soccer balls, and basketballs adorned the crib. A mobile with stylized cars hung above it, and a rug with Thomas the Tank Engine's face smiled on the floor.

Jen hugged Faith hard and rocked her gently back and forth. Finally she stepped back. "My offer still stands. I'll come and box it all up anytime you want me to. Just say the word."

Faith grabbed a tissue from the dresser. She wiped her eyes and blew her nose, then tossed the tissue into the waste basket that displayed floating aliens and large rocket labeled *Blake*. She led Jen back into the hall. "I'll be okay. I'll sleep in that one." She nodded to the room beyond the bathroom. "Thanks for coming. You're the best bestie ever."

\* \* \*

After locking up behind Jen and brushing her teeth in the main bathroom, Faith tiptoed into the upstairs guest room. It would be hard to sleep in this room—she never had. That's if she could sleep at all. Rather than turning on the ceiling light, she shuffled her way to the nightstand and pulled the lamp's chain. A dim yellow glow spread into the room, revealing the earth tones of the comforter and the dark oak finish of the heavy bed frame and matching nightstands.

Faith slipped out of her clothes, folded them, and laid them over the foot board, then pulled on her nightgown. The two pillows in their shams lay askew against the headboard, and the brown and tan jacquard stripes of the comforter undulated erratically. It had been a while since she'd cleaned in here.

Isme liked to hang out here with Maddie where they could both lie crosswise on the queen bed, playing Minecraft or Plants vs. Zombies Heroes on the iPad. Isme called it the Retro Room. It was the only room in the house that had escaped the scrupulous interior decoration that Faith had applied to the rest of their home. Instead, it contained the furniture and bedding from the master bedroom in their first home—a small apartment. Faith had often wondered whether Isme's subconscious memories attracted her to this room. Perhaps this bed, like an emotional homing beacon, still emitted the comfort of snuggling between Daddy and Mommy for two a.m. feedings during her first year of life.

Faith set the pillow shams on a chair, crawled between the tan sheets, and reached toward the lamp. A tumbler with an inch of water in the bottom sat on the nightstand. No doubt Isme had brought a full glass in here a week or more ago after being told to hydrate and had taken only a sip. Evaporation had consumed the rest. Faith shook her head. Getting that girl to stay hydrated required eternal vigilance.

When she pushed the glass aside, she noticed a framed photo behind it. Her heart stabbed. It was a wedding photograph of her and Lance holding hands and staring, enraptured, into each other's eyes. She lifted it from the nightstand and held it in her hands as she lay on her side.

Lance's joy matched her own—his half of the picture looked like a bridal magazine cover. She still couldn't get over having landed a man as good-looking as Lance. Studying herself in the photo, she compared her image to Katrina's flattering portraits. Her own over-sized mouth, elongated chin, and uncooperative blonde hair were plain at best—no match for Lance's male model looks. She certainly lacked a model's curves —curves Katrina had. But, judging by the devotion in Lance's eyes that the photograph captured, all that hadn't mattered to him back then.

Now, evidently, he wanted more.

Why was this picture here? It was usually in the family room—or had she moved it to Lance's office? Isme must have been looking at it, maybe showing it to Maddie for some reason. She liked to show off her father to her friends. Still clutching the photo, Faith pulled the lamp chain and lay stiff in the darkness.

With her heart still twisting painfully from Lance's betrayal, she pressed the photograph to her chest like a poultice. She wasn't ready to give up on him—or their marriage. Katrina might be accustomed to taking first place—but not this time.

*Reconciliation.* The word Jen had repeatedly spoken echoed in Faith's brain. This didn't have to be the end. If only for Isme's sake, Faith would somehow find it in her heart to forgive Lance. As long as he repented of his affair and promised to stop the porn.

And if he wouldn't? Perhaps he knew he had all the power in their relationship. He made all the money and had all the prestige. Being divorced wouldn't hurt him—he could get any woman he wanted. Rich, handsome, successful, smart. He had it all, with or without Faith.

# Chapter 3: Pumpkinseeds from Deephaven

Despite the picturesque parks, lakes, and blooming suburban neighborhoods that rolled past her car windows, Faith saw only gloom. She'd donned her happy mommy face at breakfast. While Isme packed her bag for her girl's day out with Wanda, Faith called first Collette and then Gretchen, using her sunniest voice. Collette invited Faith to join her, the boys, and their au pair for fishing and a picnic. On her way home, Faith would meet Dr. Gretchen at the Landscape Arboretum for an afternoon walk.

Remembering the promise she'd made to Jen, Faith fought off the desire to call Lance as soon as Wanda and Isme drove away. With effort she resisted the urge to crawl back into bed to hibernate and cry all day. She'd remain calm and follow the plan she'd made with Jen.

Faith pulled onto Collette's parking pad and stepped out onto the concrete. From this side of the house the home looked deceptively simple, like a single-story cottage with gray-and-white brick exterior. But Faith knew better—the magnificent side of the three-level home faced the lake.

She took a deep breath. Was she ready for this? Even under normal circumstances, Collette's overwhelming personality, like ginger or garlic, was best consumed in moderation. Faith had let Collette talk her into joining this family outing—a situation she couldn't easily extract herself from if it grew uncomfortable. But it would be worth it to find out what Collette knew about Lance and Katrina.

Although Collette was more than an acquaintance, she wasn't someone Faith would bare her soul to. Certainly Collette's inevitable *I told you so* would sting, but she wouldn't let it rile her. No matter what she learned, she'd keep her cool in front of Collette.

She rang the bell, and Sophie answered.

"Good morning," said Sophie in her lilting German accent.

"*Guten morgen*, Sophie." Faith stepped into the entry. "*Wie gehts?*"

Sophie smiled and tossed her long blonde hair. "*Sehr gut. Ich freue mich dich wieder zu sehen.*"

Faith shrugged and laughed. "I'm glad to see you, too?" She'd already used up most of the German she knew.

Collette waved from the kitchen's center island as she stuffed sandwiches into an Igloo cooler on the floor. "We're just about ready. I'm so glad you called. Are you wearing your suit?"

Faith patted the beach bag at her side. "It's in here."

Collette snapped the lid of the Igloo shut. "Better change now. Use the powder room." She nodded toward the other side of the dining room. "We've got ours on already. Sophie! Time to get their sandals on!"

Crossing the dining room, Faith let her eyes scan the open great room beyond. She sucked in her breath. She could never get used to the beauty of this home, which was something right out of HGTV glamour edition. On both sides large windows lined the walls, and at the far end, a curved wall of windows opening onto a balcony looked out over the glimmering blue lake—a stunning view in all four seasons, but especially at the height of summer. Kneeling on the floor between crimson semicircular couches, Collette's two sons played at a round wooden train track.

When Faith emerged, they all trekked down two levels. After skirting the pool, they followed the pavers down to the private sandy beach. Trailing his mom, four-year-old Aiden bounced and skipped onto the dock, tugging on Sophie as two-year-old Gabe toddled at her side. Faith, rolling the cooler at the rear of the procession, paused to admire the high-end speedboat and luxury pontoon parked under a double awning. Collette and Steve certainly had it all.

They piled into the pontoon. After Collette backed the boat out, she idled the engine while she slathered her neck and arms with sunscreen. She tossed the bottle to Faith. "This is the best stuff. No parabens."

Faith rubbed it on her arms and legs, then applied some to Aiden's skin. He giggled, and Faith tousled his ginger hair. What a cutie.

Collette eased the boat into St. Alban's Bay, heading toward the bridge. Though the day couldn't be better—there wasn't a cloud in the sky, and the sun was warm but not overpowering—Faith's insides fluttered. She wouldn't be great company when all that filled her head was the image of Lance with another woman. How would she ever get a chance to talk to Collette with the kids and Sophie around? She was regretting this already.

Spreading his little legs wide like a seasoned sailor, Gabe toddled over to Collette. She drew him onto her lap, letting him hold the steering wheel with her. He grinned, but before long he twisted and squirmed, trying to get more space on his mom's lap, which was nearly nonexistent because of her large belly.

Collette set him down, and Faith motioned to him. Dropping his blond head, he looked up at her shyly through his thick lashes. Suddenly a grin spread across his face like the sun breaking through the clouds. He trotted toward her, and she gathered him onto her lap. As his little boy fragrance laced with sunscreen warmed her nostrils, she relished the pressure of his stocky little legs.

He was about a year older than Blake would be now. He felt heart-wrenchingly good.

Soon he wriggled away and went to kneel on the forward bench by Aiden and Sophie. Since Collette was intent on steering between other craft, Faith followed him and knelt at Aiden's other side, peering at the vista ahead. As the boat moved into open water, Faith and Aiden pointed out passing boats and swooping birds to each other. Now they could see just how big Lake Minnetonka was. When you were in one of its many bays or inlets, it looked like any small Minnesota lake. But it was huge. Looking ahead and to the left, Faith could barely see the opposite shore.

When a speed boat zoomed past, the wake set the pontoon bobbing, and Aiden gripped the back of the bench and whooped. Gabe copied his every move. Standing to Gabe's right at the forward gate, Sophie steadied him with her left hand. With her golden hair blowing free in the wind as she tilted her chin upward, she looked like a carved Norse warrior maiden decorating the prow of a Viking ship.

Faith summoned her courage—she could be fierce and noble, too. She should at least start the dialogue with Collette. She moved astern and positioned herself on the seat across from the captain's chair, leaning forward so she didn't have to shout.

"It's invigorating out here."

Collette closed her eyes and inhaled deeply. "I love it!"

Faith focused on the water ahead. Driving with one's eyes shut on the lake might not be as risky as on land, but it couldn't be a good idea.

Collette opened her eyes and corrected course, turning the steering wheel left. "Have you heard from Lance?"

Faith shook her head.

"No biggie." Collette tossed her head. "Steve hasn't called me yet, either. You know how the gala is. Always goes late." She chuckled. "Remember how bored we were in St. Louis last year? The AAW—Association of Abandoned Wives?"

Faith laughed, too, but she recalled the event differently. Collette had alternately amused and scandalized their group with tales of her youthful escapades in Europe—crazy things she'd done before she met and fell in love with Steve in Switzerland.

Collette nodded toward the bow. "We're heading for Big Island. We'll eat lunch there. Then we can give the guys a call."

As a speedboat passed, rocking the pontoon, Faith's stomach flipped. Normally she was immune to seasickness, but not today.

Soon Aiden pointed straight ahead and shouted, "Land ho!"

Collette aimed the boat for one of two docks jutting out from the wooded shore of the island. A couple of pontoons and a few simple fishing boats bobbed in the water nearby, their occupants quietly chatting. As Collette maneuvered the craft inches from the dock, Sophie hopped out and tied a mooring line to a pole.

Collette shut the engine off and stood, motioning the boys toward her. "Who's hungry?"

Putting thoughts of the upcoming phone call from her mind, Faith opened the cooler and handed out cans of stevia-sweetened soda. Collette tossed a bagged sandwich to each person, and Sophie set a plastic container on the smoked Plexiglas coffee table. Faith eyed it curiously.

"*Kartoffelsalat*," Sophie explained, lifting the lid.

"Potato salad!" Faith laughed. "Did you make it?"

"*Ja!* It's my mother's recipe." She scooped some onto a plate and handed it to Faith. "*Authentischer bayerischer Kartoffelsalat.*"

"Authentic Bavarian," Collette translated. She popped a forkful of the golden potatoes with flecks of red onion and chives into her mouth and chewed with obvious delight. She smiled at Sophie. *"Das schmeckt sehr gut!"*

Faith sampled it. The warm temperature and sweetly sour taste surprised her, but it was pleasant. *"Sehr gut!"* she mimicked. Then she nibbled the sandwich. She feared the little brown bun would taste like cardboard, but it tasted sweet and nutty. Peeking inside at the contents, she saw what looked like ham, Swiss cheese, avocado, and sprouts.

She took a full bite and savored it. "Mmm. Where do you get these buns?"

"We made them—me and my helper." Collette gave Aiden, who sat beside her, a squeeze. "Wheat free. We grind our own spelt flour."

Aiden nodded, wide-eyed, but couldn't reply —his mouth was jammed full.

When they were nearly done eating, Collette's cellphone rang, and Aiden scrambled to dig it out of her day bag.

"Hi, honey!" Collette's eyes sparkled as she updated Steve about their morning. She gave Faith a knowing look, then spoke playfully into the phone. "Faith wants to know if Lance is being a good boy."

Faith's jaw dropped. She hadn't exactly told Collette why she wanted to get together, but she must have figured it out. She blurted it out to Steve like a joke—when it was dreadfully serious.

Evidently Steve had a detailed response. Collette's expression turned grim. She mumbled "mmmm," and "uh-huh," and "oh" as she kept her eyes on Faith. Faith's heart dropped to her stomach. Were Lance and Katrina making a spectacle of themselves? She envisioned Kat's long, bare arms curled around Lance's neck as they danced to slow and sensuous music in the glitzy ballroom.

Gabe tugged on his mommy's dress, and she

held the phone out to him. He plastered it to his ear and paced back and forth across the deck like a tiny executive, nodding gravely to whatever his daddy was saying. Faith smiled despite her curiosity. She was dying to hear Steve's news about Lance.

When her own cellphone rang, she jumped nearly a foot off the seat. It was Lance's ringtone. For a moment she panicked—she couldn't talk to him. He could just leave a message. But Sophie rushed to Faith's beach bag, found the phone, and handed it to her.

She answered.

"I left a message earlier." Lance's voice sounded cheery. "We're just heading into our afternoon workshops. How are you?"

Faith clenched her jaw as she stepped out onto the dock and walked toward shore. "Fine." She reminded herself of her promise not to confront Lance over the phone. She had to stick to the plan. "How was the gala?"

"Boring, as usual. Too many self-important people trying to impress each other. I miss you."

Faith's heart thumped in her chest. His voice sounded so sweet, so intimate. She steeled herself. "How did you sleep?"

"Like a log."

Her abdomen constricted as if she'd been punched. Because of his sexy bunk mate? Trying to catch her breath, she wandered onto shore and followed a paved path under the trees. Bitterness welled up, and she couldn't resist taking at least a mild jab. "Too much wine?"

There was a long pause at Lance's end. "What?" He sounded confused.

Though she regretted saying it, his pretense of naiveté rankled. "I'm at Collette's. We're on the lake having a picnic."

"What a coincidence." Surprise came over the phone. "Steve's talking to her right now. I didn't know you two were planning on getting together."

"We all have our little secrets, I guess."

Iciness crackled from her voice. When he asked about her talk with her agent and about Isme, she answered in short, clipped fragments. Finally he said he had to get to his workshop, and he sounded hurt. Good. Let him feel the burn.

When Faith returned to the boat, Collette was attaching a lure to a fishing line. At first no one looked at their guest, giving Faith time to regain her composure.

When he noticed she'd returned, Aiden bounced up and down. "Daddy told me to catch a northern for him, and I said I would."

"We'll try." Collette arched her brows at him. "But the fish might not want to be caught, you know."

Aiden tilted his head as if a new thought had just hit him. "Then how do you ever catch one?"

Collette laughed and cast the line.

Sophie ruffled Aiden's hair. "Your bait must be *wirklich unwiderstehlich*." At Faith's questioning glance, she translated, "Truly irresistible."

A shock passed through Faith's body as she gingerly lowered herself onto the seat. She pictured the bottle of Truly Irresistible Chablis and Katrina posing next to the fountain. Her stomach felt sour. The delicious meal wasn't sitting so well.

Collette let Aiden turn the reel to wind in the line. After casting it several more times with no success, she shook her head at Aiden and shrugged. "They're not hungry right now. It's not the best time for catching northerns. We'll try for pumpkinseeds when we get closer to home."

Aiden seemed ready for something new. "Can we go to the beach?"

"You betcha."

Collette stowed the rod while Sophie untied the line. As Collette started the engine, she eyed Faith with pursed lips as if willing the words she wanted to speak to remain sealed for now. They rounded the point of the island and motored out into open water again. Before long Collette maneuvered the pontoon between two tiny islands, each crowded with boats at docks, then pulled into a narrow bay and docked at Deephaven Beach.

Sophie flung the kids' bag over her shoulder and grabbed the boys' hands. *"Los geht's!"*

Quickly Collette strode after her and stuffed the sunscreen in the bag. "Look for us in about an hour."

As soon as they had passed the two little

islands again and headed into another narrow bay, Collette locked eyes with Faith. "Steve says he tried to keep tabs on Lance at the gala, but he didn't want to be too obvious. Eventually he lost track of him, and he found out that both Katrina and Lance had left the party. That doesn't necessarily mean anything. Lance told him this morning that he turned in early."

Faith instantly broke into a sweat. She fanned herself with her sun hat. "So Steve thinks there's something between them."

Collette shrugged, holding both hands palms up for a moment before she returned them to the wheel. "I'll fill you in when we stop. Just on the other side of that bridge."

They motored under a bridge, and Collette shut off the engine, letting the pontoon drift in the quiet, shallow inlet. She motioned to Faith to join her on the rear bench under the canopy.

"You know Steve's the partner in charge of HR, right?" At Faith's nod, she continued. "He made the final decision to bring Katrina on, and he's regretted it almost since day one."

Faith hadn't expected Collette to speak so directly. Things must be dire. She shifted uncomfortably. "Why?"

"You know how strict their sexual harassment policies are. Employees can't date other employees or clients. But ever since Katrina came on board, she's been hitting on Lance." As Collette placed her hand on Faith's arm, her bicolored irises seemed to penetrate Faith's soul. "I tried to warn you a month ago."

Faith blinked back tears. "I know. I was stupid." She swallowed hard. "Is it just Lance she's after?"

Collette nodded slowly. "She's very slippery. She keeps her flirting just under the radar. Steve's been documenting little things, but it's all so subtle, he hasn't been able to call her out on anything yet. That's why he was watching them so closely at the gala. He figured she might slip up at the convention, and he'd nail her."

"And Lance."

For the first time Faith realized this affair could jeopardize her husband's position—not just his marriage. Maybe he did have something to lose after all.

"Lance is a partner." Leaning back against the seat, Collette put her feet up on the table and stretched out her long white legs. "But that doesn't mean the rules don't apply to him. Since the beginning, all the partners have committed to following office policies like everyone else. If they disciplined Katrina, Lance would have to get the same treatment. Otherwise it wouldn't be fair."

Faith's mouth went dry. "Has Steve talked to Lance about her?"

"Nope. He has no evidence yet—just a strong gut feeling. He says there's way too much chemistry between the two of them."

Faith wiped the sweat from her forehead.

"Should you be telling me this?"

Collette puffed her hair out of her eyes as if blowing off any strictures of propriety. "I'm not an employee, am I? Besides, I've seen it, too. But don't tell Lance that Steve has talked to me about it. He probably shouldn't have, but we share everything with each other."

A pang shot through Faith's chest. Collette and Steve had the close relationship that she and Lance used to have. Would she ever have that feeling of complete unity with him again? Once a couple lost that, could they ever get it back?

She screwed up all her nerve. She might as well confirm her suspicions. "So you think they're having an affair?"

Lacing her fingers atop her belly, Collette tilted her head from side to side as if debating what to say. "Let's just say I wouldn't be surprised. I don't like it that they both went missing from the gala. It might have been the opportunity she's been waiting for."

Faith wouldn't reveal what she'd found in her bed. The opportunity had apparently already presented itself with her trip to Wisconsin Dells. She should never have gone.

"I'm really sorry to tell you all this, Faith. But forewarned is forearmed, right?" Collette's eyes and expression softened. "If it was going on with my husband, I'd want to know the truth. You can't fight what you don't know. And the sooner you put a stop to it, the better."

Faith stared at the trees on the shoreline. Her heart ached, and her limbs felt limp. "Do you think Lance was ripe for the picking—he wanted to be caught?"

Without answering, Collette looked at her watch and hopped back into the driver's seat. "We've got to get back."

They traveled in silence to the beach. Faith could only assume Collette's failure to answer meant yes. When they pulled up to the dock, Faith hopped out and tied a line as Sophie had done.

Collette motioned her back on deck. "We can't leave the boat here long, or we'll get a ticket." She stepped out of her sundress and tossed it on the captain's seat. "But we can take a quick dip to wash the sweat off."

Faith pulled her sundress over her head, folded it, and tucked it into her beach bag. Collette was already on the dock tying her red hair back with a thick scrunchie. The paisley-covered apron of her swimsuit clung tightly to her beautifully rounded abdomen. Whether she'd get another month from it seemed doubtful. Faith's chest squeezed painfully. The last time she'd been that pregnant was ten years ago. Blake hadn't made it to eight months.

Collette hurried her with a wave of her hand. "Come on!"

Following Collette past the sign that said *Loading and Unloading Only*, Faith strode down the dock as if it were home turf. In her teens she'd worked as a lifeguard for two summers, and being around water always boosted her confidence. She looked forward to a quick swim to calm her nerves. She'd gotten a good tan so far this summer, and the padded cups of her swimsuit added some shapeliness to her straight figure. No one would consider her well-endowed, but at least she was fit.

When she passed the lifeguard she felt a stab of guilt for violating the boat dock rules. The young woman wouldn't notice the pontoon, though —the crowded beach consumed all her attention.

Sneaking up on Aiden and Gabe in the kiddie area, Collette splashed them playfully, and they clambered into her arms. Faith swam out beyond the ropes, heading for the raft with a powerful freestyle, but she could hardly take three strokes without running into other bathers.

"Fa-aith!"

Collette, Sophie, and the boys were on the beach, gathering their things. Faith swam to shallow water and ran to meet them.

Back on the boat, they all sat under the canopy out of the sun, now high in the sky and beating down relentlessly. As they got under way, Sophie made the boys drink water, but Gabe was clearly exhausted. He kept grinding his fists into his eyes and yawning. Faith wrapped him in a beach towel and set him on her lap, and within a minute, he was asleep. Leaning against Sophie's arm, Aiden closed his eyes.

As they motored along, Faith tried to

concentrate on Collette's conversation as she bemoaned the lack of diversity at Deephaven Beach. "There wasn't a brown or black face to be seen." She swung her arm around in a panoramic gesture. "Deephaven's as lily white as it gets, and Greenwood, our little town, is the same. Not sure how these boys will ever meet anyone of color."

First world problems, Faith thought, though this could be a way to attract Collette to Christianity. Their church was pretty diverse for a suburban Minnesota fellowship. But Faith was in no position to suggest church to Collette—not when Collette's marriage was thriving and hers was floundering.

Soon they passed under the first bridge they'd come to and motored back into St. Alban's Bay. Collette looked around at the boys. Sound asleep on Faith's lap, Gabe didn't stir, but Aiden must have sensed the slowing of the engine.

He popped up, blinked, and rubbed his eyes. "We're gonna catch pumpkinseeds, right, Mom?"

Nodding, Collette gave him a thumbs up. After they puttered to their left beside a wooded peninsula that extended into the bay, Collette cut the engine. Enjoying the rare chance to cuddle with Gabe, Faith was content to sit and watch for a while.

Collette pulled out three bamboo rods and a container of worms. She helped Aiden bait his hook while Sophie baited hers. They made short casts into the water off the port side toward shore.

Aiden peered at the water, focusing on the bobbers. "I got a bite!"

"Reel it in slowly," Collette instructed.

The little rod arched, and Aiden pulled back on it as he continued to reel. Soon a small yellowish fish burst through the water. Collette reached for the line and swung the struggling fish onto the deck. She extracted the hook with a needle-nosed pliers and dropped the fish into a bucket.

Aiden crouched beside it. "It's a pumpkinseed, isn't it, Mommy?"

Squatting next to him, Collette peered into the pail. "You're right! How can you tell?"

"'Cuz it's shaped like a pumpkin seed and has a fake eye!"

Aiden pointed at the bright red spot next to a large black dot at the end of the fish's mouth. Throwing his shoulders back as he straightened, he looked at Sophie and Faith for praise.

Faith grinned at him. What a smarty pants.

Setting down her pole, Sophie's eyes met Aiden's. "*Und auch?* What else do you know about this fish?"

Crinkling his brow, the boy thought for a moment. His eyes lit up. "The daddies make nests in the mud with their tails and watch over the babies." He faced Faith like a little professor. "We saw a movie about it. The daddy carried the baby back to the nest in his mouth. I thought he was gonna eat it, but he was making it stay home."

Faith laughed. "Really? They *are* good daddies, then."

"Every woman's dream man." Collette winked at Faith. "He builds a beautiful home and takes care of the kids." She drew in her chin at how Gabe was plastered against Faith's chest. "You can lay him on the bench, you know."

Rocking the sweaty, sleeping boy, Faith shook her head. "Not a chance."

Sophie caught Aiden's eyes and pointed at the shiny, speckled fish. *"Sie haben ein großes Untugend."* Collette motioned to her to continue. "Their one big—how does one say?—vice. *Sie haben großen Appetit*—big appetites." She rubbed her stomach as if ravenous. "So they nibble any worm that passes. This one took the bait—so quick." She snatched at Aiden's nose, and he drew back, giggling. "We must think *mit unserem Kopf,*" she tapped her temple twice, *"nicht mit unserem Bauch."*

She tickled Aiden's middle, and he squirmed away.

Collette arched her brows at Aiden. "Think with your head, not with your tummy!" She laughed and turned toward Faith. "You don't get much meat from one of these little guys." She pulled another worm from the bait container. "Most people toss them back, but we'll have them for supper." She handed the baited rod back to Aiden. "They taste good—just a lot of work to fillet. But without predators, they'd overpopulate and spread disease in the lake."

Faith smiled politely at the conservation lesson.

As they continued fishing, Collette, Sophie, and Aiden all reeled in more of the panfish and plopped them into the pail. Reclining with one arm around the toddler, Faith had a perfect view of the captured creatures. Their false eyes with the brilliant flash of red were a gift from their Creator. To a potential predator fish, the placement of the false eye would make the pumpkinseed appear four times its size, so the little fish avoided conflicts it couldn't win.

*Wise as serpents and harmless as doves.* The Bible verse came to mind, and Faith shook her head. She had been foolish to talk to Lance the way she had. She wasn't going to resolve this conflict over the phone, so she should have treated him normally. Now he might suspect she knew something, and he had plenty of time to craft an alibi. She needed to think with her brain, not with her wounded heart.

She felt sorry for each gasping fish that ended up in the bucket—especially now that she knew what good daddies they were. Lance, too, was a dream husband. He had provided her with a home beyond her wildest expectations, and he was wonderful with Isme. But like the fish, he had a vice—an appetite that had led him into trouble.

When Gabe began to fuss, Collette started the engine. In a couple of minutes they arrived at her house with its distinctive rounded façade and dramatic rectangular pillars. As Sophie took the boys to shower and change into clean clothes, Faith planned how to quickly yet graciously take her leave.

But when they reached the kitchen and Faith set the Igloo down, Collette beckoned her toward one of the black leather bar stools at the second kitchen island. By the glint in her eyes, Faith could tell she wanted more one-on-one time. Realizing she wouldn't get away so easily, she settled herself at the counter.

Collette sidled onto the stool next to Faith, propped both elbows on the granite, and cradled her chin in her laced fingers. Her smile poked fun at herself as the golden centers of her blue-rimmed irises sparkled. "Now, far be it from me to pry."

Faith stiffened for whatever onslaught Collette had in mind.

"I know you guys were having fertility issues —you'd been trying for a long time before you got pregnant again, right? Was it Lance's problem, or yours?"

Heat crept into Faith's face. Leave it to Collette to bulldoze into personal territory. But she had been so kind, Faith couldn't feel offended. "The specialists said it was Lance."

Collette nodded knowingly. "He's got quite the sweet tooth, right? And a coffee habit?"

Faith set her jaw. Here came the nutrition lecture.

"Deadly combo for sperm count."

"All his blood work is within normal limits." Faith willed herself not to roll her eyes. "His specialist didn't think his diet was a problem."

"Hah!" Collette guffawed, then slapped her hand over her mouth. "Sorry! Specialists." Lowering herself from her stool, she let her eyes roll. "Don't take my word for it. Do your own research." She stepped toward a six-foot high cabinet door along the cupboard wall and opened it, revealing rows upon rows of supplements. She picked out two bottles and set them in front of Faith. "If you're trying to conceive again," she tapped one bottle, "have Lance take this one." She tapped the other. "You take this one. No charge—they're on me."

Faith eyed them skeptically.

Collette took Faith's hand in hers and stared into her eyes. "You'll get through this. Lance is a good man, and you two are awesome together." She squeezed reassuringly. "Lots of couples survive affairs."

Faith's eyes widened. Suddenly Collette's tone had changed, and she sounded as if she spoke from experience. But Steve was crazy about Collette—he could never have—

"Everyone deserves a second chance."

Was that guilt that flickered in her eyes?

"Mommy! Can we have a popsicle?"

Collette grinned at the two little boys rushing toward her. "You betcha!"

# Chapter 4: Assassins at the Arboretum

When Faith arrived at the Landscape Arboretum, it was a few minutes ahead of the time she'd texted Dr. Gretchen, so she followed Three Mile Drive around the wooded outer grounds. So far the day had given no real answers, but plenty to obsess about—not the least of which was her unanswered question that still dangled maddeningly. Did Lance *want* to get caught by the sexy Katrina? And if so, why? Why would he betray her this way and throw away his family and marriage? Could she have prevented this somehow?

She thumped her fist against the steering wheel. That wasn't the point. Lance was responsible for his actions, no matter how irresistible the bait. Her forehead throbbed. She had to clear her mind, stop recycling the same repetitive thoughts. She cranked up the classical music on the radio.

As she neared the parking lot by the Sensory

Garden, she startled at the sight of three enormous ant sculptures that appeared to be marching along the road. She parked facing the third one. The menacing creature stood ten feet tall with a body more than twice that long. Six spindly wooden legs supported its three-sectioned body made from bent willow branches—like gigantic rustic baskets. Eyes of polished red cedar glared from behind its wooden antennae. Isme would freak out if she saw these sculptures—she despised ants.

Gretchen's teal Malibu with its KIDSDOC license plate pulled into the lot. Wearing running shorts, an aqua racerback tank top, and Nike running shoes, Gretchen hopped out of her car. After greeting Faith, she suggested a trek around Green Heron Pond and set out in an energetic stride, leaving Faith to catch up to the bobbing light brown pony tail.

When Faith synced with Gretchen's pace, Gretchen eyed her curiously. "So, is Isme still lying?"

"I need to apologize for that." Faith launched into her prepared answer. "I gave you the wrong impression." She explained the bank hacking that coincided with the coyotes incident. "I was trying so hard to find another explanation, but now I've accepted that Isme sees visions."

"Visions?" Gretchen sucked on her lower lip thoughtfully. "As Christians, we shouldn't be surprised by that, I guess." They reached the boardwalk and followed it as it skirted the wild grasses of the pond. "What's that verse? God's ways are higher than our ways and past finding out."

Relieved at Gretchen's words, Faith let her shoulders relax. She had feared that Gretchen, as a woman of science, might object to such things. "I think I know what God was trying to tell me."

"Oh?"

Faith recounted Isme's second vision about the black cat and her discovery of a black hair in her bed. Shame burned her cheeks as she spoke. She hated to tell on Lance and admit their marriage was failing, but she could trust Gretchen to be discreet.

They reached the end of the boardwalk and retraced their steps. Gretchen's expression was noncommittal. "What does Lance have to say?"

"He's out of town for the weekend at a convention—I found the hair about an hour after he left."

"You can't call him?"

Faith stopped and, placing her hands on her hips, faced the doctor. "When you get a lab report of a malignant tumor, do you tell the patient over the phone?"

Gretchen shook her head, obviously grasping the analogy. "We deliver that kind of news face to face."

"Exactly." Faith began walking again. "Lance can tell me in person what he's been up to—so I can see him squirm. And he can see the pain he's caused firsthand."

Their footsteps echoed along the boardwalk as they finished the trek in silence. The sun, though sinking, still scorched.

"Couldn't there be some other explanation?" Gretchen placed a hand on Faith's back, guiding her towards a bench under some spreading maples. "Maybe you're blowing this out of proportion."

"Like those ants at the entrance?" Faith let out a rueful laugh. "Yeah, my life feels like a B-grade horror flick from the fifties right now."

She dropped onto the bench and studied her hands in her lap. "But it's time I was honest with myself. Plenty of people tried to warn me about my marriage—but I ignored them."

Sitting beside her, Gretchen drew in her chin. "Really? Who warned you?"

She was playing naïve—probably to protect patient confidentiality, as Jen had predicted. Faith would have to prod delicately to extract Gretchen's information. "Collette—her husband works with Lance. They've both noticed a lot of 'chemistry' between Lance and Katrina."

Gretchen nodded slowly, encouraging Faith to go on.

"And his mom." Faith cast her gaze across the pond. "I'm going to talk to her tomorrow, but she seemed to be hinting at something." She turned her eyes on Gretchen. "Even you tried to warn me."

Gretchen rose to her feet. "Let's go to the waterfall garden." She nodded her head to the left.

"It's just down there."

After following a path along a stream, they came upon a rocky area with a Southwest ambience and several waterfalls. Atop the highest one, where water tumbled down over a twenty-foot cliff, another massive insect stood watch. A giant cedar damselfly perched on a stand of bleached driftwood. Showing through the open lattice of the wings, weeping willows against the azure sky created the appearance of green-and-blue stained glass.

The two women sat on the rail of a low log fence facing the gigantic creature.

Faith nodded toward the damselfly. "Another humongous insect. I sense a pattern."

"It's some kind of traveling exhibit." Gretchen studied it. "There are ten different big bugs placed around the park." She must have felt Faith's eyes resting on her expectantly, and finally she cleared her throat. "Of course, you know that even if Lance said something to me that suggested you were having marriage problems, I wouldn't be able to share that with you because of HIPPA privacy rules."

Faith nodded, but she could tell Gretchen wanted to reveal more.

"I can only share general observations from my experience and training." She considered the damselfly in silence for a full minute. "Sadly, I've had several patient families in my practice who've had a stillbirth or lost an infant or older child. In med school we prepared for situations like those. Sometimes after the loss of a child, women can withdraw from their husbands. So men sometimes ask their physicians how long it takes for a woman to regain her interest in romance."

Faith's blood seemed to stop pumping. Though Dr. Gretchen had phrased it as delicately as possible, Faith was horrified to think that Lance would have asked her such a question. Gretchen was single. How could she possibly know what it was like to try for years to conceive, only to lose the child seven months into the pregnancy?

Lance had last seen Gretchen months ago for blood work. Even at that point, evidently, he was chomping at the bit. He wasn't willing to give his wife even a year to work through the worst pain of her life. Men, it seemed, had only one thing on their minds no matter what else was going on. His selfishness pierced her heart.

Faith stiffened and crossed her arms over her chest, glaring at the plantings of yucca and prickly pear cactus among the rocks flanking the water fall. "So you're telling me I'm to blame for Lance's infidelity?"

Gretchen gently touched Faith's shoulder. "I said nothing of the kind."

Faith pulled away, scooted farther down the fence rail, and glared at her companion. "But that's what you're implying. I thought as a woman you'd be more enlightened. But it's always all about the man's needs, isn't it? The woman's needs don't matter. And if the man strays, it's her fault for not keeping him interested."

Her voice was too loud, causing several people walking past to turn to look at them, but she didn't care. She flung her arm toward the damselfly. "Talk about blowing things out of proportion! Maybe I've been a bit withdrawn; maybe I've shut him down a few times. But that's nothing compared to him drinking, looking at porn, and having an affair."

She buried her forehead in her palm and kneaded her eyebrows with her fingers. Despite Faith's harsh words, Gretchen remained silent and motionless. Lifting her eyes toward the falls, Faith let the rushing water soothe her. Slowly the heat drained from her cheeks.

Extending nearly the width of the pool, the damselfly's body, made of a single log, captured her attention.

*Remove the beam from your own eye.*

She shook her head vigorously. Surely that didn't apply when your husband was having an affair. With her jaw still clenched and her body stiff, she glared at Gretchen.

Gretchen dropped her eyes. "I'm not married, and I haven't lost a child." She scuffed at the gravel under her shoes. "I can't say I know what you're going through. I only meant that if what I said applies to you, you're not alone. Grief is hard on a marriage." She raised her eyes to Faith's. "Maybe you guys should go to therapy."

"We tried that." Faith shuddered at the memory. "You recommended that support group for parents who've lost a child, remember? We only went once. It was the most depressing thing I've ever experienced."

"Really?" Gretchen tilted her head. "You never told me about it."

Faith stood and wandered down the path toward the falls. When Gretchen caught up, Faith said, "The couple who ran it had lost their only daughter in a car accident years before. She was eight years old."

She positioned herself as close as she could to the falling water. A light breeze wafted the refreshing spray onto their faces and arms. "They vowed they'd never have another child—so they could keep her memory sacred." As she rubbed her upper arms, spreading the soothing water droplets over her skin, her anger cooled. "Just the opposite of me. I still want another baby."

"Did they make you feel that was wrong?"

Faith sighed. "They taught us that the only correct response to someone who's grieving is to listen to their story and say, *I'm sorry for your loss.*"

She stepped back from the water fall and began strolling the path again toward some flower beds. Gretchen flanked her.

"I agree with that," Faith continued. "But they wouldn't allow us to say anything to try to make the other parents feel better. We couldn't even talk about how we hoped for another child."

"Hmmm." Gretchen studied the blossoms along the peony walk. "It sounds like they had lots of dos and don'ts."

"They did." Faith tried to let the perfume of the flowers infuse the bitter memory. "You can't mention your hope of Heaven or say that the child is in a better place. When I shared a verse from Psalms that helped me, they scolded me—told me I wasn't respecting the grieving process."

Gretchen's eyes widened. "I had no idea."

"I swore I'd never go back there." Faith stopped in front of a fragrant bed of pink peonies and fingered a silky blossom. "But I took away two things. First, that parents who lose a child have a much higher chance of getting a divorce."

Gretchen pursed her lips. "They told you that?"

Faith nodded.

Gretchen shook her head. "That's an old myth." She rolled her eyes. "People still say that all the time. But it's just as likely that a couple will grow closer through experiencing loss together."

"Really?"

Faith considered that idea. It certainly hadn't been the case for her and Lance.

Gretchen motioned her toward the left branch of a fork in the path. "What was the second thing you learned from the group?"

They moved into a shady spot. A few kids were playing tag on a grassy circle under the towering body of a daddy long legs sculpture.

"That everyone grieves differently." Faith leaned against a tree. "They told us to give our spouses space to grieve in their own way and not expect them to grieve the same way we do."

An odd feeling crept into Faith's shoulders and neck—a deep ache that wanted to be comforted but suppressed itself. The feelings she'd had right after losing the baby. So much sorrow, so much anger, so much guilt.

Under the giant insect an older boy chased down a little girl, who was probably about six, and slapped her on the shoulder. She screamed and tore after first one child and then another, but they zoomed out of her reach. Her freckled face contorted in frustration. Soon she crumpled onto the grass and buried her head in her hands, sobbing. An older girl ran to her side, knelt down, and tried to hug her, but the little girl squirmed away angrily.

"Oh, wow." Faith laid her hand on Gretchen's arm. "I know what I did."

Gretchen's eyes questioned.

Faith couldn't believe she'd never seen it before. "That's why I pulled away from Lance— because of what they told us. I was so worried about ending up divorced if I didn't give Lance space to grieve that I let Blake's death wedge us apart." She dropped onto a nearby boulder, and Gretchen sat beside her on another. "I didn't want to be clingy—too needy—because then he wouldn't do his own grieving. He'd be all wrapped up in comforting me. That's what sent us on separate paths. We've been growing further apart ever since."

"I'm so sorry, Faith." Gretchen took Faith's hands in hers and met her eyes. "It sounds like I sent you somewhere that did more harm than good. Will you forgive me?"

Faith's eyes stung. Gretchen was asking for forgiveness, but Faith had treated her abominably. "It's not your fault. You didn't know." She squeezed Gretchen's hands. "I'm sorry I blew up back there. You've always gone above and beyond what we can expect from a doctor."

"Come on. Let's look at the annuals." Gretchen led Faith onto a path that curved to their left. Brightly colored pansies, petunias of every color and stripe, tall fuzzy cleomes, sunny marigolds, and cheerful zinnias greeted them. As they walked, Gretchen seemed deep in thought. Finally she spoke. "I'm so glad you told me about your experience with that group. It helps confirm what I think God wants me to do."

"What's that?"

"I'm starting our own grief support group at church—with Ryan Peltier."

Color crept into Gretchen's cheeks at the mention of the name. An attractive father of three, Ryan had lost his wife last summer.

"Ah!" Faith arched her brows. "Is there something between you two besides this partnership?"

Gretchen smiled coyly. "We're kicking it off in September—the group, that is. I was hoping you'd join us—maybe even as our assistant."

Faith felt her heart closing up. She couldn't be part of another grief support group and dredge up all that pain.

Gretchen must have noticed Faith's withdrawal. She bit her lower lip and placed a hand lightly on Faith's arm. "I know this feels like bad timing now. I wasn't going to mention it until you brought up the group I sent you to."

Faith nodded, but felt tears welling up and couldn't speak. Bad timing was an understatement. She could only deal with so much pain at once. Her baby, her husband—what would she lose next?

She focused on the annual bed that loomed ahead. In the middle of a riot of colorful asters sat an over-sized insect made of polished cedar. Its body balanced four feet off the ground on six bent legs, its back was studded with spikes like a dragon's tail, and from its chin dropped a fearsome pointed appendage that almost touched the ground.

She drew closer to the wooden creature. It offered a way to change the subject. "Assassin Bug." She read the sign and shrugged at Gretchen. "Never heard of these."

"I have!" Gretchen shuddered. "I met one up close and personal when I was in Texas for med school." She stepped from one side of the sculpture to the other, examining it with an expression of fear and awe. "I made the mistake of picking it up. See that sword?" She pointed to the appendage hanging down from its head. "It stabbed me—over and over before I could toss it away. It hurt like crazy!"

Faith let a weak laugh escape through her teeth. "And I thought Minnesota mosquitoes were bad."

"A mosquito bite tickles compared to being jabbed with an assassin bug's sword." Gretchen shook her hand as if still feeling the sting. "But at least they don't seek humans out like mosquitoes do. They hunt other insects, pierce them, and suck out their body fluids."

Faith examined the sculpture and finished reading the placard, then moved along the path past more annual beds. She felt Gretchen's eyes on her back. She expected some kind of reply about the support group. Faith would just say no. Gretchen would have to find someone else.

"You know that day you called about Isme?" Gretchen sidled closer, breaking the awkward silence. "If I sounded surprised to hear from you, it was because I'd actually been thinking of you earlier that day. So I really hoped you'd call me at home that night."

"I'm sorry." Faith winced. She'd been so wrapped up in her own concerns that day, and so embarrassed about wasting Gretchen's time, that she'd missed the sincerity of Gretchen's offer. "I thought you just meant to call if I wanted to talk about Isme, and I didn't want to bother you any more than I already had. Why were you thinking about me?"

"I'd just had supper with my dad the night before, and we were talking about my twin sister." They walked along the path, taking in the brilliant orange, yellow, and maroon daylilies. "You probably didn't know I had one."

Faith eyed her with surprise. "I've only heard you mention your brother. Where does she live?"

"She died at birth."

Faith's heart stabbed. "Oh. I'm so sorry."

"I never even knew about her until I was a teenager." Gretchen's voice grew husky, and she blinked a few times. "My mother refused to speak of her or her death and forbade my dad to, either."

Wide-eyed, Faith shook her head.

"But after they divorced, he finally told me about my twin—Lily." Gretchen found a bench and sat, and Faith lowered herself by her side. "My dad said Mom became a different person after my sister's death—not the one he married. She was so sour and critical. Living with her was toxic—so he found someone else. Mom died of cancer while I was in med school. It was as if her grief sucked her life away."

"Like an assassin bug." Faith's heart ached. For Gretchen, her mother, and her father. "That's so sad."

"It is." Gretchen wiped her eyes with her slender fingers. "I've often wished I could rewrite my mom's history. Change it to what God meant it to be."

"I know that feeling."

"We can't do that, but we can do the next best thing."

Gretchen's plaintive expression made her even more attractive. Faith wondered that she had never married. No doubt her intense studies and career had left little time for dating.

"That's what Ryan and I have been talking about."

Faith motioned for her to go on.

"We've gone out for coffee a few times." Gretchen's face grew pink again. "He's been praying about how to turn his wife's death into something meaningful—a way to use his grief to help others."

"I can't imagine how it would be to lose a spouse and have to raise three kids alone." Faith felt a pang of shame. "I can't even get over the loss of my baby, who I didn't even get to know. But he lost his wife and his kids' mom."

"Don't minimize your sorrow." Gretchen touched Faith's arm. "His loss is horrible, but at least he has the memories of the good times to hold onto. You're grieving the lost possibilities, the memories you never had."

Gretchen had described it so perfectly. Faith's chin twitched, and she inhaled shakily. "Just like you. Grieving the twin sister you never knew."

Gretchen swallowed hard. "I told Ryan about

Lily and my folks. We realized we each had a piece of the grief spectrum. He lost a wife; I lost a sibling at birth. We started brainstorming about running a grief support group. Neither of us would be able to do it alone, but together we think we can handle it."

Faith ignored the prodding in her heart. "That's brave of you."

"What we could really use is the perspective of a bereaved parent." Gretchen's eyes bore into Faith's. "That's why I thought of you."

Faith paused before an array of red, white, and blue striped petunias. She pictured Blake's room, as untouched as a private shrine. "I might do more harm than good. I haven't handled Blake's death very well."

Gretchen bit her lower lip, and her eyes grew soft. "You don't have to be healed yet. Just on the journey and willing to grow. Having someone as a leader who hasn't healed yet shows that it's safe for anyone. We just want to be authentic Christians, doing life together, meeting people where they're at. No pressure. Just try the first meeting. Sometimes the best way to help yourself is to try to help others."

Faith wished she could be as selfless as Gretchen, but she felt her body going numb again. She didn't know what the next six weeks would bring—if she'd even have a marriage by the time the group started.

She shrugged. "I'll think about it."

Gretchen accepted that answer. They strolled past more flowers, crossed the street, and walked through the peaceful Japanese Garden. As they followed jagged white paving stones through the shady area, coolness washed over them. The splashing waterfall and the carved granite lanterns gave the space an ethereal feel.

Exiting the garden into an area of hostas, Faith shuffled along. What did her future hold? Healing —or just more pain? Suddenly she gasped. There in front of her was a four-foot-long spider clinging to a twelve-foot circular web—all made of bent willow.

She laughed, embarrassed by her groundless fear. "Not good for people with arachnophobia!"

"Actually, it might be." Gretchen stepped back and considered the sculpture. "This would be great exposure therapy—when you want to confront your fear head-on."

"Like what I've been doing this weekend." Faith focused on the wooden web and the fearsome arachnid. "I decided to stop whistling past the graveyard."

Gretchen tilted her head quizzically, then her eyes brightened, and she smiled with understanding. "Speaking of therapy again, I think you and Lance need marriage counseling, too— assuming you both want to stay together. Not just grief support."

"You're probably right. I haven't thought that far ahead."

"*This time* I won't lead you astray." Gretchen punctuated her promise with a bounce of her pony tail. "Ryan told me he and Liz went through a rough time, but they had a terrific counselor who helped them. I'll get you the name."

As they went their separate ways toward their cars in the parking lot, Faith felt suddenly drained. Heat blasted her when she opened her car door and slid into the driver's seat. She rolled down the windows and turned on the air, then quickly hopped back out, remembering a question she'd wanted to ask Gretchen. She waved down Gretchen's Malibu.

With a look of surprise, Gretchen stopped the car and lowered her window.

Faith held up her index finger. "I meant to ask you. Do you know anything about how sugar and caffeine affect men's fertility?"

Gretchen seemed taken aback. "I'm not a fertility specialist."

"I know!" Faith crunched her features apologetically. "It's just that Lance's specialist told him not to worry about his diet, but someone told me sugar and caffeine are a deadly combo for sperm count."

"I *have* seen some research on that." Gretchen pursed her lips, as if choosing her words carefully. "Dr. Grant is pretty old school. They've brought a new doc into that practice, though. Maybe Lance should switch to him." She looked upward in thought. "His name escapes me right now. I'll text it to you."

Back in her car, Faith cringed at her double *faux pas*. She'd asked her doctor friend for personal health advice away from the office—and she was worrying about Lance's fertility issues when their marriage was in trouble. As if their whole meeting hadn't been awkward enough, she'd ended it on this note.

Faith sighed and pulled her cellphone out of her bag to check for messages. Isme might have called. Her stomach dropped when she saw two missed calls from Lance and one voicemail. She didn't want to listen, but she couldn't ignore it. There could be some sort of emergency.

She tapped the play arrow, then held the phone to her ear.

"Hi, honey. Sorry I missed you. I've had a hard time concentrating this afternoon because you sounded like you were mad when we talked. I know Mom was taking Isme for the day, so I hope she didn't hurt your feelings by something she said. She can be infuriating, but she means well. And she loves you—almost as much as I do. If you want to talk, call me anytime. It's just hospitality suites tonight, so I'll be making the rounds. But I can talk whenever you want. Love you! Bye!"

Holding the phone against the steering wheel, Faith replayed the message. How could he sound so sincere? So concerned? He was starting to build his alibi already: He was the loving husband, she was the angry wife. How she wanted to trust him, to fall into his reassurances, believing that everything would be fine. But she knew better. He couldn't deceive her anymore.

She threw the phone on the passenger seat, crumpled against the steering wheel, and sobbed out a waterfall.

# Chapter 5: Wounding Wanda

"Ew!" Isme shrieked and threw her trowel onto the grass. She stood and backed away from the hole she'd been digging, shivering her shoulders and arms. "Yuck! I struck an ant hill!"

Faith and Wanda, still on their knees in the hosta bed, laughed as they eyed the dozen red ants that scurried over the dirt-encrusted tool.

"They're just ants, honey," Wanda crooned. "There are bound to be a few ants in a flower garden. You just have to get used to them."

Isme swatted a mosquito on her arm and waved away gnats from her face. She shivered again. "I think I have to go in now. I've got an online play date."

Faith waved Isme away. The sooner she was gone, the sooner Faith could ply her mother-in-law with questions about Lance.

Wanda sprang to her feet. "Just a minute, young lady." She stepped to Isme's side. "Online dating at your age?"

"Nana!" Isme sighed, looking heavenward and raising her hands in a sassy shrug. "It's just some girls from church."

"If you're online, you can't be sure." Wanda

squinted and wagged her finger. "There are plenty of stalkers who pretend to be friends but turn out to be creepy men trying to kidnap ten-year-old girls." She turned to Faith. "You're letting her do this?"

Swallowing a laugh, Faith stood and brushed the pebbles and dirt from her knee pads. "It's okay, Nana. It's not online, online. They just connect with each other over the Xbox. They have to know each other's passwords to join the game."

"Not passwords, Mom," Isme corrected. "Gamer tags."

"Whatever." Faith wiped sweat from her forehead with the back of her hand. "The point is, there's no way for a stranger to join."

She raised her eyebrows at Wanda, whose face relaxed.

"Well, parents can't be too careful these days." Wanda put her arm around Isme's shoulders and squeezed. "Do you have time to bring us something cold to drink—since you're abandoning us to the ants and mosquitoes?"

Isme turned and started running to the house, but her relieved voice trailed backward. "Ice tea or lemonade?"

Faith waved her onward. "One of each!"

Mentally Faith began rehearsing the questions she'd prepared for Wanda. As the two women patted the dirt around the hosta they had just planted, Isme returned with the perspiring bottles. The second Faith brushed off her hands and took the drinks, Isme made a bee line back to the bug-free zone.

Faith motioned Wanda toward the double lawn glider. In unison they ripped off their knee pads, the Velcro strips resounding through the muggy air. Steadying themselves as they sat on the swaying benches, they faced each other. Each drew a long swig from her drink.

Faith studied Wanda's shiny but dirt-streaked face. She'd let her hydrate before she dropped her first question. Wanda's frosted, short-cropped hair was darkened with sweat, and her thick eyebrows —so similar to Lance's—tilted inward, wrinkling the bridge of her nose. Suddenly Faith realized that her mother-in-law was studying her face as intently as she was studying Wanda's.

Wanda spoke first. "Now that Isme's gone inside, there's something I want to talk to you about. You know I'm not one to beat around the bush. So I'm just going to lay it on you."

Faith crossed her legs, despite her sticky skin. She'd have to let Wanda get this off her mind before she addressed the issue of Lance. Was she in for a lecture about Isme's online behavior, or had Isme spilled some secret yesterday that Wanda wanted to confront Faith with?

"Go on." Faith brought her lemonade to her lips and sipped.

Linking her fingers together around the iced tea bottle on her lap, Wanda maintained eye contact. "I have reason to believe Lance is having an extramarital affair."

Faith gasped, and the lemonade went down the wrong way. Launching into a coughing fit, she struggled to screw the lid back on the lemonade bottle. As she slammed it down on the slatted cedar seat, tears streamed from her eyes.

Wanda half rose, extending a hand to Faith's arm. "Are you okay?"

Faith attempted to speak, then coughed again. She took another sip of lemonade and leaned back against her seat, setting the glider in motion. "Sorry. Yes, I'm fine. You took me by surprise."

"Did I?"

Surprise wasn't the word. Shock. Horror. Devastation. Those might be closer. Her mother-in-law's forthright declaration had confirmed all her fears. Faith attempted a weak smile. "You couldn't tell?"

Wanda dropped back onto her bench, refreshing the glider's sway, her eyes fixed on Faith. Evidently she was waiting for Faith to ask for more.

Faith looked toward the house. No Isme. She took a deep breath. "What makes you think Lance is cheating?"

Wanda arched her brows and pursed her lips. "If I tell you what I know, will you tell me what you know? Together, we may be able to put an end to this sooner rather than later."

Faith squinted. "Put an end to…?"

Wanda clicked her French-tipped nails on her

tea bottle. "The affair, of course. Not your marriage! Goodness!"

Faith's head was still reeling—whether from oxygen deprivation, confusion, or the rocking of the glider, she couldn't tell. "You want me to tell you what I know?"

"So we can fight this together. Pool our resources. Form a united front."

Faith sensed Wanda's sincerity and recalled Lance's words: *She loves you almost as much as I do.* She could see it was true. Wanda was ready to take Faith's side against her own son—at least in order to save their marriage. But Wanda was bargaining. Why? Apparently she assumed Faith was reluctant to confide in her. True, their relationship had never been close. Wanda often rubbed Faith the wrong way. Faith had tried to be a good daughter-in-law, and she appreciated much about Wanda, but she didn't know if she could ever be close to her. No doubt Wanda had picked up on that, sensing some reticence on Faith's part, some wall between them.

Faith nodded. "Of course. You go first. What do you know?"

Wanda set her empty bottle onto the bench beside her. She leaned forward. "It's *the look*. The look in his eyes. I'd recognize it anywhere."

Faith drew her hands down her cheeks. This was Wanda's big revelation? This was her proof? She shook her head.

"I know, I know." Wanda held up both hands

as if to shield herself from imminent scorn. "You think that's not much to base my suspicions on. But I'd lay odds on it— ten to one."

"What *look*? What are you talking about?"

Wanda glanced toward the house to confirm they were alone. "It's time you learned about *the look*. I'll tell you, but it's kind of a long story."

"Should we go inside?"

Wanda jiggled her head. "No—no. I don't want Isme to overhear. This is not for little ears."

"I'm listening."

"The first time I saw the look, I was too young to know what it meant." Drawing a deep breath, Wanda brushed her hair away from her face. "But the second time, Lance was six years old. Marty and I had been married seven years. You've heard of the seven-year-itch? I always thought that was some kind of joke, or just a Marilyn Monroe movie, but it was real for Marty. That's when he had his first affair."

Faith felt her jaw drop. She pictured her father-in-law: staid, steady Marty. On the elder board at his church, active in the Lions Club, loving grandfather, devoted husband. She knew he'd traveled a rough road for a while with his alcoholism, but she'd never heard of any infidelity.

"Marty was unfaithful?"

"Yep. It was his secretary—they carried on for over a year, and I saw *the look* in his eyes the whole time. But before you judge him too much, I have to tell you how I drove him to it—because I can see it happening with you and Lance."

Faith clenched her teeth. Here it came. Wanda was going to blame her for Lance's wandering eye. She opened her mouth, but Wanda interrupted.

"Hear me out. Sometimes—you may not have noticed it—" she winked, "but I can have pretty severe bouts of verbal diarrhea. It was worse back then. I wanted a big family. You know I have six siblings. I especially wanted a daughter. But after Lance was born, nothing—year after year. And not for lack of trying. I knew it was Marty's fault, and I took jabs at him—even in front of our friends—because I was angry. So he looked for someone who made him feel like a real man."

Faith's chest tightened. Wanda had never spoken of her and Marty's fertility issues before. "How did you know it was Marty's problem? Did you see a fertility specialist?"

Wanda's lip curled down disdainfully. "Didn't need to. All the men in Marty's line are one-hit wonders. He's an only, and his father's brothers have one child apiece. And I knew I was Fertile Myrtle."

Faith drew in her chin, recoiling from Wanda's crass assessment. "How?"

Wanda sighed and looked away toward the woods beyond the yard. Eventually she turned her eyes to Faith again. "That goes back to the first time I saw *the look*."

Faith gestured for her to continue.

"I was sixteen—a junior in high school. There

was this older man who came into the burger shop where I worked—so handsome, so suave. I thought the look in his eyes meant he loved me." Wanda snorted. "He was only looking for a one-night stand. But he got more than he bargained for— because I got pregnant."

Faith was glad Wanda was staring at her own garden clogs so she couldn't see the shock on her daughter-in-law's face. Now she understood why Wanda wanted to trade information. She was revealing the darkest secrets of her life—secrets Lance had never mentioned. He might not even know about this himself.

Wanda raised her eyes. "Did you ever notice how Lance's birthday is exactly nine months after Marty's and my anniversary?"

Faith nodded.

"See what I mean?" Wanda patted herself on the chest twice. "Fertile Myrtle."

Faith's head was swirling. So many questions swam about. Before she could process the information, she blurted out, "Lance has a sibling? Boy or girl?"

"Maybe I had an abortion."

Faith curled her hands around the cedar bench beneath her. Would Wanda have done something like that as a pregnant high schooler? In a moment she knew the answer. Of course. She had worked for political campaigns that vociferously favored "choice." Faith felt her cheeks grow warm, and she finished off her lemonade without looking at

Wanda.

"But I didn't." Wanda's hoarse voice was barely audible.

Faith looked toward the older woman, whose eyes were shining with tears. "You didn't? You had the baby?"

Wanda brushed the tears away. Her chin quivered. "He wanted me to terminate. Kept pushing for it. He was a married man—a professional man. I could have ruined him. He offered to take me to the clinic, said my parents would never have to know." She bit her lower lip and let out a trembling sigh. "In the end, my folks and I agreed to keep it hush-hush, and he paid for me to travel to Florida and live with Aunt Julia during my senior year. I think he probably paid my parents a hefty sum toward my college education, but I could never get them to tell me the details. Aunt Julia helped me arrange a private adoption. I never held the baby—I barely saw her. She went to a good Christian home—that's all I knew."

"A girl. Lance has a half-sister somewhere."

Wanda nodded. "In Florida."

Faith's head felt like it was going to explode. "Does Lance know? Have you been in touch with her?"

Wanda stepped off the glider and signaled for Faith to follow. They strolled toward the swimming pool. "She contacted me a year ago wanting to meet me. I guess I authorized release of my information after she turned eighteen. I'd kind of forgotten that—I signed so many papers, and I was so young. Besides, Anna's almost forty now. I never expected to hear from her."

"Did you meet her?" Faith couldn't understand why they hadn't heard about this yet if Anna had made contact a year ago. But one question at a time. This was obviously hard for Wanda to speak of.

They reached the pool. They entered through the gate, and both women took off their shoes and sat on the textured concrete with their feet in the water.

After wetting her hands, Wanda rubbed her neck and upper chest. "No. I told her not to contact me again. She pushed so hard to know whether she had siblings that I told her about Lance. But I warned her not to contact him."

"Warned?" Faith put her hand to her forehead. "Warned?"

Wanda's face hardened. "It was right after you lost the baby. I told her it wasn't a good time and she'd better not try to track him down."

Faith's heart twisted, but her anger rose. "That should be Lance's call, not yours."

Certainly Lance would want to know he had a sister and at least speak with her. She studied Wanda's face. How could she reject for a second time the daughter she'd given away?

Wanda flicked her foot, splashing water toward the center of the pool. "No, it was mine. We didn't need any more drama. Life was hard enough. I wasn't going to have that put on Lance, too."

"Are you sure you weren't just protecting yourself from embarrassment—and using Blake's death as an excuse?"

Faith regretted the stinging words as soon as they left her lips. But she wouldn't allow Wanda to hide behind the stillbirth—not when she had willingly severed all ties with her own flesh and blood.

Wanda glared. "Do you think it's easy to give up a child you carried for nine months? I did it for her—because I knew I couldn't care for her. I was still a child myself. It was one of the most selfless things I've ever done. I was sobbing my guts out when they took her away. Maria—she was the woman who arranged everything—finally got me to calm down by telling me about a vision she had of me with another baby girl. She promised me God would give me another girl to fill the hole in my heart. I didn't even know if I believed in God back then—but I trusted her vision. Which was why I was so angry when Marty couldn't give me a daughter." Wanda bent over and filled her cupped hands with water and splashed her cheeks. "So angry that I drove him right into the arms of another woman."

What an ordeal for a mere girl. Yet Wanda had never spoken of it. She had effectively buried it—which must have made it all the harder to hear from her daughter after forty years. Faith reached over and placed her hand on Wanda's back. "I'm so sorry you had to go through all that. But why wouldn't you want to see Anna now—if she wants to meet you? Don't you owe her that much?"

Wanda frowned. "There's no possible upside. If she had a good mother and father, then she doesn't need me. She has a family. If she had a lousy upbringing, I'd feel guilty, but I know I made the best decision I could make at the time. I don't need to go through all that guilt again. And if I found out she has any of her father's wayward genes, I'd regret having perpetuated his vices." She waved her hand to dispel the thoughts. "Nothing to be gained."

Faith swirled her ankle in the water. "I'm sorry that woman's vision didn't turn out to be true. I'm sure she meant well."

To Faith's surprise, Wanda's pursed lips spread into a wide grin. "But it did come true." She held her arms as if cradling a baby. "The first time I held Isme, I knew God had made good on that promise after all. Just not in the way I'd expected." She laid her palm on her chest. "That hole's been filled for ten years now." She touched Faith's arm tenderly. "I know how badly you want another baby, but you should learn to be content with Isme. Blake was a miracle that was too good to be true. I can sell everything in his room on *Craigslist* and donate the money to whatever charity you want."

Rising to her feet, she rubbed the small of her back and extended a hand to Faith. "Let's get the last of those hostas planted."

Leave it to Wanda to set a jumble of emotions swirling. Faith didn't know whether to be mad at Wanda, sorry for her, or grateful for her confidences and empathy. But now that Wanda had shared some of her most intimate and painful memories, Faith owed it to her to share her own suspicions about Lance—as much as she hated to do so.

Suddenly she remembered something Wanda had said. "Wait! Marty's *first* affair? It happened again?"

"Mmm-hmm."

They reached the hosta bed. After strapping on her knee pads, Wanda dropped to the earth. "His secretary gave up on him—got tired of being the other woman. We patched things up, and it went pretty well for the next ten years. Although he continued to drink more and more. But it all blew up during the 2000 presidential campaign. When Lance was in high school."

"I know things were rough then, but I thought it was because of Marty's drinking. Lance never mentioned Marty having an affair."

Wanda plunged her trowel into the dirt with vigor. "We managed to keep it from him, I guess. I'm glad of that."

"He still doesn't know?"

"No."

Again Faith marveled at her mother-in-law's willingness to confide in her. She could have shared this information with Lance when she began to see *the look* in his eyes.

Wanda spoke to the ground as she dug. "I started noticing the look again, but I was so wrapped up in my work, the excitement of the campaign, that I ignored it. It was the first time I'd had a meaningful job, and I was making pretty good money, too. But for very long hours—twelve to fourteen hours a day. I wasn't home much. Marty was laid off, which I thought was perfect. He could fill in at home, and between his unemployment check and my income, we were doing better than ever. But his ego couldn't take it. He met some floozy at a bar and started spending all his time with her. I'd find out he missed Lance's debate meets, and I'd freak out. He just drank more and more, and *the look* got deeper and deeper."

She leaned back, sitting on her heels, her trowel poised in midair. "I tell you, their egos are so fragile. You gotta stroke 'em. And you gotta be there for them, to meet their needs. All their needs. Every night if necessary. Or someone else will. That's the only way to combat *the look*."

Faith's stomach soured. What a sick, sick lesson Wanda had learned. She sat back on her heels as well and squared her shoulders. "That's bunk, Wanda! Marty chose to cheat on you. *He* behaved like a spoiled child. He refused to let you have your day in the sun. It was only temporary—the campaign was going to end in November. He could have been patient with you. But he broke his vow to forsake all others and keep himself only for you. That was his fault, not yours! You shouldn't have blamed yourself."

Faith flushed, and she fanned her hand in front of her face for air. She had never spoken so forcefully to Wanda, but her blood was boiling over Wanda's unenlightened attitude.

Wanda raised her chin and leaned toward Faith but responded evenly. "So *you* say, but you'd be wise to learn from my mistakes. It takes two to ruin a marriage, and one to save it. Do you want to save your marriage or not?"

"If I have to grovel and take the blame for something *he's* done—no!"

Faith stabbed her trowel into the dirt. But instead of sinking into the ground, it hit a rock. Soil and pebbles sprayed up and flew toward Wanda's face.

"Ah!"

Wanda screamed in pain, and her hand flew to her left eye. She curled forward, clutching her eye and groaning.

"Wanda! Did something hit your eye?" Faith scooted to her side and slid her arm around the woman's back. "I'm so sorry!"

Wanda groaned in reply, rocking back and forth with pain.

Faith placed her hands under Wanda's arms and pulled her to her feet. "Let's get you inside and take a look at it."

Faith guided Wanda into the house and into the main floor bath. As Wanda hunched over the sink, Faith ran cool water and splashed it onto Wanda's face, clearing away the streaks of dirt.

"How does it feel?"

Wanda let out a string of curse words as she tried to open her eye. She braced herself against the sink. "Hurts like h—"

"Nana!" Isme appeared behind them in the doorway. "What happened?"

Faith turned and shooed Isme out the door. "Nana got something in her eye. Don't worry about it. She'll be fine."

She pushed the door shut and locked it.

Faith handed Wanda a towel. "Here, wash your hands with soap. I'll find some saline." She washed her own hands, then dug in the vanity drawer and pulled out a bottle of saline solution and a first aid kit. "Okay, we need to wash the eye out. I'm going to have to touch your eyelid, but I'll be careful."

Wanda bent her face sideways over the sink. Faith pried the eyelid open and squirted saline into the eye. Wanda flinched and yelped, then blinked several times.

"How's that?" Faith asked. "Can you open your eye?"

Wanda's left eyelid came upwards slightly, and she nodded.

"Can you see anything?"

"It's blurry, but, yeah, a little."

Faith opened the first aid kit and poked around inside. "Here's an eye patch. Do you want that? Then I'll take you to Urgent Care."

Wanda straightened and shook herself. "No! Never patch an injured eye!" She batted the eye patch from Faith's hand, and it landed back in the case. "Worst thing you can do. Bacteria thrive in the dark. Light and air kills them."

Faith gritted her teeth. Of course she knew eyes shouldn't be patched—she'd only meant to offer comfort. But she didn't blame Wanda for being angry. And scared.

Wanda reached for the doorknob. "I'll drive myself to Urgent Care. Getting too close to you can be dangerous."

Faith rested her hand on Wanda's wrist and blocked the doorway. "Wanda, I'm so sorry! I got carried away. I didn't mean to hurt you."

Wanda dropped her hand from the doorknob and sighed. She drew Faith into a hug. "Of course, you didn't." She patted Faith's back. "But you are a force to be reckoned with." She backed away and smiled. "Lance better lock up the trowels!"

The two women exited the bathroom laughing. Faith convinced Wanda to call Marty to drive her to Urgent Care, and Wanda insisted that Faith stay home with Isme. While they waited for Marty, Faith positioned Wanda in the recliner in the lower level library with an ice pack wrapped in a tea towel over her swollen eye. Wanda suspected it was a scratched cornea, which she'd experienced before. Nothing serious, she claimed, but she'd get it checked out. In a few minutes, Faith joined her with two steaming mugs of tea. The lower level was chilly from the air conditioning, so she spread a throw over Wanda's legs.

Faith thought Wanda might be dozing, but after a few minutes she drew the ice pack away from her eye and glared at Faith.

"Don't think you can get out of telling me what you know by attacking me." She grinned. "You still owe me."

Faith bit her lower lip. She'd hoped Wanda had forgotten. "There isn't much really," she began. "Just that there's this new junior counsel, Katrina Williams, who's been flirting with Lance. But there's no proof that it's gone further than that."

She felt her face flushing and her heart pounding. What she had said was true. Why should she share her possibly groundless suspicions with Wanda? That wouldn't be fair to Lance.

Wanda's expression declared vindication. "No proof but *the look*. When was she hired?"

"Three or four months ago."

"I knew it." Wanda smiled smugly. "That's when I noticed he had the look."

Faith sipped her tea. She refused to say more despite Wanda's intense gaze.

"Just a minute. I'll bring you to her." Isme's voice echoed from the top of the stairwell, and a moment later she bounded into the library carrying

Faith's cellphone in her extended hand and mouthing, "It's Daddy."

Faith felt trapped. She couldn't look at Wanda's face, and she dreaded taking the cellphone. But she accepted it and held it to her ear. "Hi, Lance."

Isme stood behind her grandmother and stroked her hair.

Lance filled Faith in on his day and his upcoming networking dinner with principals from a Chicago firm. When Faith told him about his mother's injury, he asked to speak to her.

After Wanda assured him she'd be fine, she passed the phone over her head to Isme. "How do you put this on speaker? He wants to talk to all of us."

Isme tapped the screen twice, and Lance's voice sounded into the room. "Can everyone hear me? My three lady loves?"

The three of them shook their heads at his overly chivalrous tone. He wanted to tell them about an idea a colleague had shared. "There's this quaint and charming bed and breakfast in Stillwater that has three-generation tea party weekends. The grandma, mom, and daughter stay together in a fancy suite, and they have special craft classes, tea parties, and all kinds of girly stuff. Maybe you three could do that next month. What do you think?"

"Cool!"

Isme was beaming and nodding, but Faith and

Wanda glanced at each other from the corner of their eyes while staring at the phone in Wanda's hands.

"Sure," Faith responded awkwardly. "Sounds great. We'll talk about it when you get back tomorrow."

They said goodbye, and Faith sent Isme upstairs to warm up Wanda's tea. When she heard the door at the top of the stairs click shut, she faced Wanda.

Wanda grimaced. "Trying to get you and Isme out of the house again. Has he ever called anything *quaint and charming* before?"

The same suspicion niggled at Faith, but she refused to let it show. She put her hands on her hips and leaned forward on the futon. "What? Are you going to tell me you can hear *the look* over the phone now?"

Wanda placed the ice pack carefully back over her eye and leaned her head back. "Are you going to tell me you can't?"

# Chapter 6: Mayhem on Minnehaha

The bracing flow of the water against her skin, the muted splashing and sloshing in her ears, and the invigorating strain of her active muscles and lungs blocked out all thought of the upcoming confrontation with Lance. Swimming laps was the perfect solution to the insomnia that had plagued Faith half the night. She hadn't slept a wink since four o'clock, so waiting until six to plunge into the pool had required great self-control. At five-thirty she'd scowled at the pink-tinged sky, denying the promised hope of the new day. Her queasy stomach and racing heart declared it to be a day of dread.

She executed a flawless flip turn, somersaulting and pushing off with as much power and speed as she'd ever displayed on her high school swim team. After completing several more laps, she hoisted herself onto the pool deck with the satisfying pounding of her heart still urging her onward. She splayed her limbs out on the nearest lounge, panting as the cool morning air raised goose flesh on her skin.

The sun had moved higher in a cloudless sky. Today would be a scorcher. Bring it on. The water had washed away her nervousness, leaving pure resolve. She would be a formidable force with Lance—a force to be reckoned with. Since he had no idea what awaited him, she would have the upper hand. For a moment she considered canceling with Jen; she didn't need her advice after all. When Lance stepped through the door, she would throw everything in his face and let the chips fall where they may. He was at fault. Why should she spare his feelings? He hadn't spared hers.

She drew her swim wrap around her, stepped into her flip-flops, and headed back to the house. With every step, her endorphin-induced confidence dwindled, and by the time she stood in front of the coffee maker, the scoop of beans trembled in her hand. What if Lance had decided on this trip that Katrina was the woman he wanted? Worse yet, what if, when he was ready to repent, facing a bitter and angry wife drove him back to the arms of the other woman? Faith squeezed her eyes shut as the coffee grinder whirred. She must get this right. Her marriage, her home, her family—her whole world—depended on it.

Steaming coffee in hand, she sat at her computer to look for recipes. "Fifteen Romantic Dinner Ideas for Your Special Someone"—that sounded promising. Red wine-braised short ribs; shrimp, spinach, and feta orzo; sheet pan steak and veggies. What would be the best way to prove her love before lowering the boom? And what would she have time to prepare and cook between her return from Jen's and Lance's arrival at six o'clock?

After perusing a dozen more please-your-lover culinary blog posts, all the options blurred together into one gigantic, stomach-turning hobo stew. Unable to decide, she created three separate shopping lists. She showered and dressed, then double-checked Isme's overnight bag that she had packed in the trunk of the car Saturday night.

From the garage she heard a vehicle rumbling down the driveway—Marty and Wanda must be arriving to pick up Wanda's car. She opened the garage door to the sight of Marty standing next to his Buick.

"Where's Wanda?" Faith glanced into the empty LeSabre. "You may be good with cars, but you can't drive both of them home yourself!"

"She's up on the road." Marty jabbed his thumb over his shoulder, gesturing up the hill toward the entrance to the development. "She insisted on feeding the crust of her toast to some ducks that were waddling across the street."

"Ducks?" Faith squinted. "Is she trying to avoid me?"

Marty shook his head, obviously amused. "Why would she?"

"She didn't tell you I was the one who nearly blinded her?"

Marty shrugged. "I heard you two had a heated discussion about Anna, that's all. Complete with mud-slinging." He winked. "But as an old political operative, she's used to that."

Faith laughed politely. Wanda hadn't accurately explained the event—probably because she didn't want Marty to know that Lance had *the look*. Hardly surprising since in Wanda's world, women single-handedly kept their menfolk on the straight and narrow without troubling them with trivialities like responsibility, accountability, and truth.

"How's her eye?"

"The ointment they gave her at Urgent Care seems to have done the trick." Marty glanced back toward the street. When he noticed Wanda descending the driveway, he placed his hand on Faith's back and guided her toward the side lawn. "I'm glad she finally told you about Anna." His voice was low, as if to keep Wanda from hearing, although she was a football field away. "I hope it didn't shock you."

"I'll admit I was surprised." She gave a little shiver. "But it's so exciting to think Lance has a half-sister. I'm sure he'll want to get to know her." When they reached the hostas, Faith stopped walking and faced her father-in-law. "But Marty— Wanda needs to meet with her."

"I agree." Marty looked back toward his wife, who was quickly shortening the distance between them. "She takes Anna's number out just about every day. She's almost called her a few times. But she's scared."

"She can't let this opportunity slip away." Faith swallowed against the lump in her throat. "She's so lucky. Not many women get the chance to reconnect with their lost child."

Marty's eyes glistened. "You should tell her that. Not today, but when she lets Lance know about Anna."

"When will that be?"

Marty patted Faith's arm. "Soon. Telling you was the first step, and that gave her courage to—"

"Investigating the scene of the crime?"

Faith and Marty both startled at Wanda's raised voice. She had reached the Buick and continued power-walking toward them.

"Just admiring our handiwork." Faith gestured toward the hosta bed. "Once they fill in, they'll be gorgeous."

Wanda looked between Marty and Faith with pursed lips, as if detecting their discussion. She nodded toward the plants. "Make sure you soak them good today."

\* \* \*

As a dart whizzed past her ear and struck the wall behind her, Faith ducked. But she wasn't the target.

"Ow! Mom! Josh stole my Nerf pistol!"

"Because you hid mine!" Another foam

missile hissed past as two of Jen's kids tussled their way into the living room.

Josh bumped into the couch, causing the stacks of folded laundry that were piled on the cushions to teeter precariously. Sarah, taller and older, wrenched the gun from his hand.

Faith looked around the small home, trying not to judge. Seven people living in a house less than half the size of her own was bound to lead to pandemonium. Normally she wouldn't care—she'd visited Jen's home many times and knew how lively it was. But today she felt her patience already slipping away. With all this going on, would Jen really have time to help plan tonight's conversation with Lance?

"Mommy, this needs batteries!" Rushing in with a remote control in one hand and an upside-down racing car in the other, Caleb collided with his older brother and tripped. The remote flew out of his hand, making a direct hit on a stack of clothing, which toppled over into the next, causing a domino effect. Soon the couch was as jumbled as a scavenged clearance table at Wal-Mart.

"Now look what you guys did!" April, who had welcomed Faith and Isme into Jen's home, rolled her eyes and looked apologetically at the visitors. Glaring at her siblings, she placed her hands on her hips. "Everyone take your clothes to your room. Then come back and set the table."

Surprisingly, April's younger siblings obeyed her without so much as a frown. The eleven-year-old was a competent lieutenant, it seemed.

As she surveyed the dirty dishes that overflowed the sink and the coloring books that concealed the dining room table, Faith suppressed a cringe. Maybe God knew she couldn't handle a brood this size—not until she tamed her OCD tendencies anyway.

"I'm so glad you could come over." April flashed a warm smile at Faith and Isme. "Mom's changing Abbie's diaper. She'll be right out." She took Isme's hand and, drawing her close, led her toward the kitchen. "After lunch our friend is coming to show us his new rabbit. And you can see all of ours."

As April updated Isme about their rabbits, Faith wandered past the reading nook where Jen held story time and into the dining room, which doubled as a schoolroom. Buying a foreclosure was the only way Jen and Tim could afford this lot with its two hundred feet of Minnehaha Creek frontage. For five years they'd lived with walls in various stages of demolition and construction, flooring being torn up and laid down, and the constant smell of paint and varnish. Faith could never have handled such turmoil.

But the result was impressive. Faith couldn't deny that in its own way the home had more charm than her own. Absently she began closing up coloring books and returning the crayons to their boxes.

"Don't worry about arranging them in perfect

order." Jen arrived at the table carrying the toddler. With one expert, continuous motion she plopped the little girl into the high chair and swung the tray in place. She swooped up a piece of paper from the stack on the bookshelf, grabbed the crayon from Faith's hand, and set both on Abbie's tray.

Faith glanced at the crayon box she held in her other hand. Sure enough, she'd sorted them by color. She felt her face morphing from peach to blush and braced herself for a taunt about her organizing compulsion.

Instead Jen tenderly touched her shoulder. "How are you? How did things go this weekend?"

Faith shrugged. "I got less than I expected but more than I bargained for."

Jen tilted her head. "What do you mean?"

"I didn't find any evidence. No notes, no gifts, no suspicious phone numbers on our bill. But—"

April bustled in and cleared away the remaining books and crayons. On her heels, her three siblings, accompanied by Isme, appeared with plates, glasses, and utensils.

Jen motioned Faith to follow her to the kitchen. "I want to hear all about it after lunch. Once we're alone."

\* \* \*

"This one's Ruby."
"And this is Horatio."
"Of course, we had to have a Peter."

Each child pointed out his or her favorite Dutch rabbit to Faith as she walked past the hutches in the expansive back yard. The elegant lounging creatures with their broad white collars seemed to belong in a Flemish Masters painting of Renaissance gentlemen.

Isme was in love. She cooed and crooned over each and begged to hold them. As April opened a hutch to draw one of the animals out, Jen called Faith over to her vegetable garden.

"Now that they're busy, tell me how it went with Collette, Gretchen, and Wanda." Jen turned up the volume on the nursery monitor she wore clipped to her shorts. She had put Abbie down for a nap while Faith and the kids cleaned up from lunch, so she was finally free to talk. "Any more clues?"

Faith let out a long exhale, blowing her sweaty hair away from her forehead. "Collette's pretty sure they're having an affair," she began.

Jen raised her brows. "Really?"

Faith continued. "Steve's been watching them, but they have no objective proof."

Now that it was time to put it all into words, her case seemed woefully flimsy.

"Hmm. So not much to go on." Jen stooped to pull a weed from a tomato cage. "And Gretchen? She probably couldn't divulge anything."

"Yes and no." Faith pulled up several more stray pieces of grass. "It sounds like Lance complained to her about not getting enough attention—of a certain kind—from me."

Jen laughed. "Nothing shocking there. Only the complaint of every man in the universe." She rummaged through the spreading vines and discovered an overgrown, yellow cucumber. "This one got missed."

Rankled by Jen's response, Faith crossed her arms over her chest and glared at her. "Giving every man an excuse to stray. You sound like Wanda!"

"Whoa!" Jen glared back. "How so?"

"According to her, *I'm* the reason Lance has *the look.* She's convinced he's having an affair because the same thing happened to her and Marty —twice—until she learned to keep him satisfied. In Wanda's world, if a woman doesn't want her husband to fool around, she'd better be his sex slave."

Jen curled her lip in disgust. She yanked the fat cucumber from the vine and pitched it into the tall grass beyond the garden. "What rot!" She shook her head. "A wife's job is to call out the best within her husband—his higher self—not merely cater to his impulses. Wives inspire their husbands to show courage. And to love. But we can't do that if we treat them like children—or animals."

The words soothed Faith's soul like a healing ointment. Too bad Wanda had never learned to see marriage that way.

As they continued to move through the garden, Faith told Jen about Lance's phone calls the past two days—so warm and convincing. She shared her suspicions about his proposed three-generation weekend in Stillwater. Then she recounted Wanda's surprising revelations, including her chance to reunite with her long-lost daughter. Finally, she told her about Collette's fertility tips and Gretchen's grief support group.

Jen let out a whistle. "I see what you mean about getting more than you bargained for."

A red-haired, freckled-faced boy bicycled into the yard.

"Hi, Jared." Jen waved at him.

He joined the children, and they swarmed around a carrier on the back of his bike.

"We know him through 4H," Jen explained. "Looks like he brought his new rabbit."

Kneeling, Faith picked a few zucchini that Jen said were large enough and laid them on the grass. Sitting back on her heels, she tucked her sweaty hair behind her ears.

Jen settled down beside her. "So you were trying to find out about Lance, but it sounds like everyone had other news to pass on to you."

"I should feel relieved that I didn't find any more signs of an affair," Faith sighed. "But I can't help thinking that it might just mean that he's really good at covering his tracks. And that scares me more than—"

Faith froze at the sound of Lance's ring tone coming from the pocket of her capris. Jen waved her hand, prodding her to answer.

Faith stood and drew out her phone. "Hi, Lance." She squinted, trying to hear Lance's voice over the background noise. "Lance? Lance?"

At Faith's signal and confused expression, Jen moved to her side, and Faith tapped the speaker icon. She turned the volume down, but both women could hear what sounded like airport terminal noise. Then a voice came through, distant but discernible above the hubbub. A feminine voice.

"Ooh, Lance, what a perfect spot," the voice purred, growing gradually louder. Faith felt her own eyes grow as wide as Jen's. The muffled woman's voice continued, "C'mere, baby." More hubbub. What was going on? "Ooh! I like that. That's good." There was a sensuous giggle. "You naughty boy!" the voice protested in the most encouraging tone possible. "Do that again! A little lower this time."

Faith's eyes stung, her face burned, and her insides swirled like a whirlpool. Lance must have pocket dialed her, and she was listening in on—what, exactly? Lance and Katrina carrying on in a corner of an airport frequent flyer lounge? The tears overflowed. She felt herself swaying. Jen moved closer, grasping her arm to steady the cell phone as it continued broadcasting its horror.

"Uh-oh. There's Steve." The voice grew louder. "Quick—take this file—before we get the evil eye again."

Suddenly the line went dead. Faith and Jen

locked eyes, mirroring each other's shock.

"Mom, look! Isn't she beautiful?"

As Faith turned around, Isme pushed a large black rabbit toward her. "Hold her! She's so sweet!"

Faith shoved her phone back in her pocket and quickly brushed away the tears so Isme wouldn't see them. But the girl was focused on the animal. Shakily Faith took the creature in her arms. Stroking the rabbit's silky, iridescent coat, she tried to erase for a moment—for Isme's sake—what she had just heard.

"Her name's Cleopatra."

The rabbit turned its blue eyes upwards.

Faith shrieked. *Blue eyes, black hair. Cleopatra.* Just like the cat in Isme's vision. Her arms flew apart, and the rabbit fell to the ground. She stumbled backwards. It bounded away.

"Mom! What'd you do that for?" Isme scolded. She screamed across the yard, "Jared! Help! She's getting away!"

"Don't panic!" Jared shouted. "Don't chase her! You'll scare her more!"

The scene shimmered and waved before Faith as if reflected in a fun house mirror. A maelstrom of little bodies darted about madly, diving at the rabbit and tripping over each other. The screams of the children played in Faith's mind like a drunken calliope. When she felt Jen's hand on her back, she crumpled to the earth, hiding her face in her hands and sobbing into them.

"I'm sorry, Faith." Jen laid her arm across Faith's back as she dropped to her knees beside her. "That was awful. We should have talked in private—inside. You don't need this ruckus right now."

Faith lifted her face, wet with tears. "*Cleopatra*." She shivered head to toe. "That's what Isme called the cat in her vision. Jen … I think I'm going to be sick! I can't take this!"

She doubled over, pressing her forearms into her abdomen.

Jen stood and pulled her to her feet. "C'mon. Let's get you out of here." She guided Faith by her elbow toward the white picket fence at the back of the lot. Beyond it flowed Minnehaha Creek. "Keep walking—right through that gate. We're going for a paddle."

She ran back toward the kids, who had cornered the rabbit. "April! We're going canoeing for a bit." She pitched the nursery monitor to her daughter. "Listen for Abbie!"

\* \* \*

Dip, stroke, lift. Repeat. In the bow of the canoe, Faith concentrated on the rhythm of paddling until her mind sequestered the memory of the phone call and her heart beat more smoothly. This section of Minnehaha Creek wound past the back yards of modest mid-century suburban homes. Although in spring it flowed fast enough to be dangerous, today it was shallow and sleepy. Occasionally, when she could see past the seaweed below, Faith spotted the muddy creek bed. From the stern, Jen steered them toward the middle of the stream whenever their canoe scraped bottom.

"Let's talk, Faith!" Jen called. "I can paddle solo for a while. You can turn around. Just take it slow."

Faith stowed her paddle. Gripping the side of the canoe as she kept her weight centered, she carefully scooted her body around to face the stern. Jen's paddle lay crosswise in front of her as she leaned to one side and the other, counterbalancing Faith's movements. She picked up the paddle again and centered the boat to the current so they could meander slowly past the tree-lined banks.

It was much cooler in the shaded waterway than it had been in Jen's garden. As the memory of the gut-wrenching phone call resurfaced, Faith squeezed her eyes shut and clenched her fists. When she opened them, Jen's concerned face urged her to speak.

Faith punched her fist into her open palm. "Now I've got some real evidence."

"Do you?"

Faith released an exasperated sigh. Did she really have to put it in words? "I just heard my husband making out with another woman."

Jen winced. "It kind of sounded like that…"

"Kind of? Good grief!" Faith gestured with both arms, causing the canoe to bob. "I'm not going to lie to myself. I'm not naïve. Any two-year-old could tell what was going on."

"Steady!" Jen swayed to keep the boat straight. "There was a lot of background noise. We had a minute of audio—no visual—"

"Visual!" Faith shuddered. "There's only so much a woman can take! Hearing it was more than enough!"

"Okay, okay. Let's see what we've got. Duck!" Jen used her paddle to push away from a huge fallen branch, and they both crouched as the canoe glided under it. "Lay out your facts one by one from the beginning, and then we'll figure out how you can discuss it all with Lance tonight."

Faith closed her eyes for a moment to gather her thoughts. When she opened them, she focused on the tall weeds along the bank as they inched past. "We'll skip Isme's visions. After those? A woman with long black hair slept in my bed. Lance has been looking at porn—and drinking."

"Whoa!" Jen jiggled the paddle in the air at her side. "A bottle of wine in the cupboard doesn't prove he's been drinking."

Faith thrust out her chin. "No? Then what does it mean? Why are you defending him?"

Jen leaned away, laying the paddle across the canoe between them. "I'm not. I'm trying to keep it factual, okay?" She raised both palms. "Just the facts, ma'am!"

Faith shook her head at the cliché. "All right. Hair in the bed. Porn on the computer. Wine in the cupboard." She counted off three fingers on her left hand. "Steve and Collette have noticed Katrina flirting with Lance—and chemistry between them. Both he and Katrina left the gala early." She held up all five fingers of her left hand. "He complained to Gretchen months ago about my lack of romance." She displayed her right thumb. "He has the look of an *adulterer*." As she spat out the word, she raised her right index finger. "And I heard him and Katrina together at the airport—doing *something*—something they didn't want Steve to see." She flashed eight raised fingers at Jen. "Those are the facts."

"Good. You're doing great, Faith. Stay calm. Let's take them one by one." Jen took off her glasses and polished them on her shirt, then put them back on. "You can talk about the porn, for sure. And you can *ask* about the wine." Biting her lower lip, she stared beyond Faith as the canoe continued to drift. "Are you free to tell him what Collette told you?"

"Probably not." Faith squirmed with irritation. "Collette doesn't want him to know that Steve talked to her."

"Okay, so that's two things off the list." Jen swiped her right index finger across the index finger and thumb of her left hand as if to erase those facts. "And you can't bring Gretchen into it —you don't want to get her in trouble." She swiped against the thumb of her right hand. "And it wouldn't be good to tell him his mom thinks he has *the look*." She swiped across her right index finger. "So—the hair, the porn, the wine, and the phone call. That's what you've got."

Jen put the paddle back into the water and straightened the canoe.

Faith drove her palms against her forehead and kneaded her scalp. It was back to square one. Suddenly she dropped her hands and jerked her head up. "The blue sheets! The blue sheets on our bed. They're still there. He can't deny those!"

Jen shook her head slightly, raising her shoulders, as if she didn't grasp the significance.

Faith slapped her hand onto the canoe seat. "They're supposed to be mauve!" The canoe listed to port, and they both wobbled their bodies to steady it.

Holding the paddle with one hand, Jen held the other up in a sign of surrender. "Fine. Ask about the sheets, too. But there's probably a good explanation for them. I wouldn't put too much stock in that one."

Faith clenched her teeth. How could she explain the violation of her color scheme and what it signified? To put blue sheets into the mauve palette irked her, stabbed her deeply in a way that defied reason, she knew. In some irrational way it was as brutal a blow as her husband's infidelity, and it all meshed together to spurn her, pierce her spirit, and negate her identity. She didn't expect Jen—whose world was so haphazard—to understand that. But Lance? If he didn't, then he wasn't the man she loved, the man who knew her and cherished her for who she was—quirks, compulsions, obsessions, and all.

"What about dinner?" Jen continued paddling. "Have you decided what to make?"

"I have now." Faith growled. "I'll throw him some scraps and send him to the doghouse."

"You don't have a doghouse."

"I can get one."

Jen chuckled. Then, growing serious, she locked eyes with Faith. "You have every right to be furious. Absolutely. But rage isn't going to serve you. You want to save your marriage, right?"

"Of course I do." Faith ran her fingers through her hair. "I've got three dinner ideas. I'll decide at the store. Once he's eating—then what?"

"We always give the couples we counsel a few guidelines. Speak the truth in love. Seek first to understand. And use *I* words, not *you* words."

"Let me try." Faith linked her fingers together under her chin and batted her eyelashes. "Lance, dear, I found a woman's long black hair in our bed and porn on your computer. I overheard you making out with a woman at the airport. This makes me want to murder you. Can you please tell me what's going on?"

Jen smirked. "That's not bad, but cut the sarcasm. Try for a normal tone of voice. And probably rephrase the murder part." She paused for Faith to nod agreement. "It's best to take one issue at a time."

"The second I see him, I'm going to hit the roof." Faith rubbed her upper arms vigorously. "I can't do this."

Jen straightened. "Yes, you can. You have to." Her expression softened. "God will give you strength in the moment. If you plan it out too much, you won't be free to listen to the Holy Spirit."

"To be honest, I don't feel God's presence much anymore." Faith slumped. "It feels like I'm on my own."

"Oh, He's there. Grace abounds more. God's building something good. He remakes our failures better than we ever could."

"Did you just compose a song?"

"Sorry! It's the bridge for one I've been working on. But really—you *must* see God's hand —giving you more than you asked for. In the grand scheme of things, your marriage problem is just a bump in the road. Yes, it's painful. But God wants to repair your marriage plus accomplish so much more."

Faith squinted at her skeptically, but Jen was on a roll.

"He's giving you a chance to help Wanda heal and grow. And with Gretchen's support group, a way to heal from losing Blake. And what if Collette's tips about fertility are what you guys need to conceive again? If you hadn't reached out to Collette, Gretchen, and Wanda this weekend, none of that might have happened. I'd say God's been working overtime for you lately."

No one could tap into the spiritual perspective like Jen. Could she be right? Was this just a bump in the road—with a happy marriage just around the bend? Faith felt a glimmer in her heart she hadn't felt since before Blake died—warmer than the July sunshine.

Jen backstroked to stop the canoe. "That's Knollwood Shopping Center there. We'd better turn around. Going upstream is slower."

Faith carefully turned to face forward again and took up her paddle. Together they maneuvered the boat against the current and paddled north. They synced their strokes. After every four dips of the paddle in the water, Jen yelled, "Switch!" and Faith rowed on the opposite side of the canoe. Against the slow current they sped along.

Soon the passing greenery blurred before Faith's eyes, and she envisioned herself greeting Lance in just a few hours. The glimmer of hope sputtered and died. Being sanguine and trusting God was easy for Jen. Except for having some financial difficulties, she'd led a charmed life. Her devoted husband was a rock-solid Christian who led marriage retreats. Every year she was either giving birth or finding out she was pregnant again. She hadn't the slightest inkling of how it felt to have your prayers denied year after year—and when they finally seemed to have been answered, to have that precious life within cruelly snuffed out.

"Ack!" Faith screamed as what felt like a cold, wet, scaly snake slammed against the back of her neck and slithered downward. She batted at it furiously and came away with a muddy string of seaweed in her hand. Looking over her shoulder, she glared at Jen. "Hey, watch it!"

Jen laughed. "Oh! So sorry!"

Faith rededicated herself to rowing. A moment later she recoiled at another splat. Thick mud oozed down her back. Jen cackled. She was doing it on purpose! Faith shivered angrily. How could she grocery shop with mud all over her shirt and bottom? She whirled partially around. "Knock it off! You're ruining my clothes!"

Jen splashed her again. This time water slapped her face, and Jen taunted. "Make me!"

Faith couldn't believe Jen's juvenile antics. They weren't in college anymore. "Okay, you asked for it!"

She dug her paddle deep into the creek bed, pulled up a pack of mud, and lobbed it toward the back of the canoe. The craft pitched wildly.

"Careful, Faith!"

It was too late. Both women went flying into the creek. Faith landed on her bottom, the murky water engulfing her. Quickly she gained her footing—the water was only waist high. She looked around for Jen and saw her face-down a few feet ahead of her. She dove toward her, flipped her over, and when she saw she was conscious, stood her on her feet.

Jen thrashed her arms and sputtered. "My glasses! I lost my glasses! Don't step on them!"

Faith steadied her friend, grasping her arms below her shoulders. A bleeding gash crossed the corner of her left eyebrow. She seemed otherwise unharmed, but she looked around frantically, panicking from her impaired vision.

"Are you okay?" Faith asked. "Jen, look at me!"

Jen focused on Faith's eyes and nodded her head. Faith didn't like the disorientation she sensed. She scanned the water for the canoe. It had floated slightly downstream and lodged against the bank. One of the paddles butted against the stern while the other was nowhere to be seen. The nearest bank, ten feet to her left, offered a fringe of sand. It was someone's yard, but no one seemed to be about.

"Let's get you to shore, and then I'll find your glasses." Faith placed her hands at Jen's waist and walked her through the water. Faith sat her down on the bank and leaned in close. "What's your name?"

She smiled weakly. "Jen, of course."

"Just checking. Stay put."

Faith waded back toward the middle of the stream and dove underwater, searching the muddy, weed-covered bottom for Jen's glasses. She pushed aside strand after strand of scratchy or slimy weeds, coming up for air again and again. Finally, twenty feet downstream from where the women had fallen out of the canoe, a sliver of sunlight glinted off a shiny lens, partially buried in muck. She dove for it and seized the glasses frame, extracting it from a slimy stalk.

Surfacing in triumph, she waved the glasses above her head. "I've got them! They look fine!"

She sloshed back upstream and toward the bank where Jen sat. She tried to clean the glasses on her own soaked shirt before passing them to Jen.

"Thank you!" Jen put them on and exhaled in relief. "I can't believe you found them!"

Flopping down on the bank next to her, Faith placed her hand on Jen's arm. "That was so stupid of me! I can't believe I did that. Can you forgive me?"

"It was my fault, too." Jen squeezed Faith's hand. "I egged you on. I was trying to get you to loosen up!"

Faith eyed her muddy clothing. She wasn't sure what had become of her flip-flops—they were probably on their way to Knollwood. Thankfully she'd left her cellphone in Jen's shed. Her capris sported an L-shaped tear at mid-thigh. Her shirt was partially unbuttoned, and underneath it the cami, sticking to her like sealskin, was plastered with fragments of seaweed.

"I think it worked!"

Both women burst into laughter. They hugged each other.

With effort, Jen tried to rise, then sank back

down.

"Hold on, dearie!" Faith chided. "You took a blow to the head, you know." She stood and pulled Jen up. After she crooked her elbow and wrapped Jen's hand around it, she began picking her way along the shore with Jen at her side. "That's good. Take it easy. Your place is just a few houses ahead, isn't it?"

Jen nodded. "The canoe?"

"It's half full of water and missing a paddle."

\* \* \*

"Shine the light toward her eyes now," Faith instructed, and little Caleb waved his Thomas the Tank Engine flashlight in front of his mommy's face.

Joshua peered at her eyes as Faith explained. "See how both pupils get smaller at the same time? That means she probably doesn't have a concussion."

Jen, wrapped in three blankets and positioned on the family room couch, smiled at her sons, who had stayed to help look after their mother while the two girls and Jared went for the canoe. Faith had bandaged her head while the boys got her a drink of water.

"One more thing, Josh." Faith whispered in the boy's ear.

Josh knelt by his mother's side, taking his EMT training seriously. "Who's the President of the United States?"

Jen looked to Faith for confirmation. At Faith's nod, she replied, "President Barack Obama —for a few more months, anyway."

Josh flung himself onto her chest, wrapping his arms around her neck. "You're right!"

When the girls and Jared returned, Faith accompanied Jen to her room. While Jen showered, Faith shut herself into Jen's walk-in closet, dried herself off, and pulled on the sundress Jen had found for her.

Jen stepped out of the master bath. "You sure you don't want to rinse off at least?"

Faith consulted her watch. "I'll shower at home. I won't have time for grocery shopping now. T minus three hours and counting." At the sight of Jen's bandaged forehead, her chest twinged with guilt. "I'm so sorry I did that to you. First I almost put Wanda's eye out, and now yours. I'm not safe to be around."

"Accidents!" Jen waved her hand dismissively. "Stuff happens."

As much as she wanted to believe that, Faith knew differently. "Both times I was angry. If I hadn't lost my temper, we wouldn't have tipped the canoe." Remembering the slimy green snake of jealousy that had slithered from her inner depths, Faith rubbed her neck with her hand. "I'm the worst friend in the world."

"No way!" Jen stepped toward her and wrapped her in a hug. "We all do things we're not proud of sometimes. That's what grace and forgiveness are for."

"You're the best BFF ever, Jen." Faith patted her back and pulled away, smirking. "And not a bad songwriter, either!"

Jen grimaced apologetically. "Did I do it again?"

Laughing, they emerged from the bedroom to find Isme and Sarah waiting for them.

"Mom! April and Sarah want me to stay overnight. Can I?"

"Funny you should ask." Faith winked at Jen. "I just happen to have your overnight bag in the trunk of my car."

"Wow, Mom!" Isme threw her arms around Faith's middle. "You must be psychic!"

As the girls dashed away, Faith muttered, "If only! Then I'd know what Lance has been up to—and how everything's going to come down tonight."

# Chapter 7: Clash over Colors

With the potatoes she'd bought at the roadside vegetable stand boiling on the stove, Faith quickly pulled a red onion from the pantry and began to chop. Bavarian potato salad wouldn't need time to chill. The brats she'd frozen after their Wisconsin Dells trip were thawing in a pan of water in the sink, and the zucchini Jen had foisted on her when she left lay on the granite, ready to be sliced, skewered, and brushed with Italian dressing. Certainly after a weekend of fancy restaurant meals, Lance would prefer a simple summer meal from the grill. She would set the deck table with their new watermelon-themed patio ware—which would coordinate with the red and green vegetables.

Perhaps she could master this take-it-as-it-comes approach to life after all. Jen's home, though chaotic, was supportive and fun. Faith blinked back the tears the onion drew. If God was watching out for her, as Jen insisted, she could afford to let go a little. She could forgive Lance as

Wanda and Jen had forgiven her, and they could move forward with counseling and a fresh start.

"Reconciliation."

She said it aloud. That was the end goal.

Lance called to say he'd be home just after six. Faith kept her voice cheerful. She was excited to see him—just not excited for the conversation they needed to have. But she wasn't going to overthink it. She'd listen for God's prompting. She'd calmly share her concerns, one at a time, and hear what Lance had to say. They would get through this.

When she heard his car pulling into the garage, she stationed herself at the door. He strode in, smiling, and immediately drew her into a kiss that was surprisingly long and passionate. She forced herself to concentrate on it rather than the specter of him kissing Katrina at the airport. After some small talk, he took a quick shower while she set dinner onto the table on the deck.

During dinner, he was animated and charming —and oh, so handsome. His dark hairline—which still showed no signs of receding—framed his forehead with the hint of a heart shape. Her eyes moved down his strong jaw to his gently squared chin. This wasn't the first time she'd noticed the suggestion of a heart's outline in his face, but it tugged on her own heart wildly tonight.

*Love me!* it said. *You know you want to.*

If it shouted that to her, could other women hear it, too? Had Katrina heard it?

She tried to focus on the highlights of his trip as he shared them, and she praised the t-shirt he'd brought home for Isme. More talkative than usual, oblivious to her internal storm, he seemed to have genuinely missed her.

His brown eyes, bordered by appealing laugh lines under his dark rectangular brows, sparkled as he spoke. They didn't look like the eyes of a man who harbored secrets. So sincere and honest, they mesmerized her. There was no black hair in the bed—it was only a meaningless vision, a vanishing fantasy. Lance was hers and hers alone.

Lance finished off the last of his brat and pushed away the remaining slices of zucchini. "That hit the spot," he groaned, stretching his legs out straight under the patio table. "It's great to be home."

Calling up the image of Katrina, Faith roused herself from his spell. Her stomach quivered, and her heart pounded in her chest, but it was now or never. She leaned forward, her forearms on the table.

"I've been pretty upset since you left."

Lance tilted his chin. "I thought something was wrong. What's going on?"

"I found porn on your computer."

He stroked his fingers across his eyebrows, then looked at Faith directly. "About that. I'm done with it. I already decided when I flew out on Friday—I'm downloading a filter tonight. And you can check my history every day. I know it was wrong, and I'm sorry. I really am."

Instead of feeling relieved at Lance's penitence, Faith felt deflated. She was stoked for an argument—this would have been Round One. But there hadn't even been any sparring. Now she felt ill-prepared for Round Two—thrown off balance by his dodge. She couldn't let him off that easily.

"Only because you knew you hadn't erased your history and I might find it."

The blow landed. He winced. "Maybe so. But I've been feeling lousy about it ever since it started. It's not who I want to be—and it disrespects you."

Faith's eyes stung, and she willed her chin not to quiver. She had to keep punching. "Ya think? It makes me feel like I'm not enough—that you need more than me." Lance reached for her hand across the table, but she pulled her hands onto her lap.

"I realize that now. I'm sorry. I mean it, Faith." He kept his hand, palm up, on the table as he continued to lean forward. "Besides, if Isme ever found out I was into porn, she'd be devastated. I won't do this to her—or to you."

He was on the ropes with his gloves down. Exactly where she wanted him. She steeled herself. "There's something else."

Lance watched with curiosity as she slid her hand under the tablecloth and withdrew a mauve envelope. She took her steak knife and slit it open. Trying for a smooth, defiant slice, she faltered, and the envelope tore from top to bottom. No matter. The hair, coiled like a viper, lay within. She passed the gouged envelope toward Lance in her open hand.

"I found this in our bed on Friday."

Confused, Lance stared at the envelope, then took it in both hands. He studied it blankly for a moment, then quickly dropped it to the table. When he looked up, Faith read the fear in his eyes, and her muscles tightened to pounce. But she waited, staring at him with bolts of ice.

"I—I can explain." He shifted awkwardly. He clasped his hands in front of him on the table and leaned toward her earnestly. "It's not what you think, Faith."

Folding her arms across her chest, she leaned away, maintaining her frigid gaze.

"A colleague—from the office—spent the night Thursday." He dropped his eyes to the cedar planks of the deck. "We had to tie some things up on a case before we could leave for the weekend."

"This *colleague* certainly has long hair." Faith tapped her nails on the table. "Doesn't she?"

Lance nodded without looking up.

"Was there a reason she couldn't take the guest room? She needed a teddy bear—a bed warmer?" Faith felt ready to erupt. She rose, shoved her chair against the table, and stormed into the house. Lance's footsteps bounded after her. He touched her arm, and she jerked away, whirling around to face him. "Don't touch me!"

"Faith! Honey! Please listen!"

As angry as she was, the anguish in Lance's voice and on his handsome face tugged at her heart. She motioned toward the family room, and they both sat, Faith in her chair and Lance in his. Glaring at him, she clenched her jaw and her fists.

Lance leaned forward, resting his folded hands on his knees. "I didn't sleep with her. She was interested in our room, and I let her stay there."

Smirking, Faith raised her eyebrows. Did he really expect her to believe that?

"I slept in the guest room."

"What a cozy arrangement." She let the sarcasm overflow. "A happy little slumber party. Tell me, who was this friend you invited for a sleepover while I was away?"

Lance rubbed his palms on his thighs. "Her name's Katrina Williams. She's a junior counsel."

"Funny, I've never heard you mention her."

"Why would I?" He slipped from his chair, crossed to hers, and knelt beside it. "She's nothing to me. Honestly."

Faith shifted to face him. "Just a drinking buddy?"

His face fell, telling her everything she needed to know. She bolted out of the chair and strode toward the window wall.

Lance followed. "You found the wine."

Looking beyond the pool toward the preserve, Faith nodded.

He touched the back of her arm gently. She

didn't pull away.

"Come sit down," he pleaded. "I'll tell you everything. From the beginning."

Leaning against opposite arms of the love seat, they eyed each other over the boundary line of the seat cushions. Lance swallowed and exhaled. "So, like I said, we had some work to finish up. I invited Katrina over—in hindsight, that was a bad idea. She brought some wine—she's been on me to develop a taste for wine so I don't stand out like a sore thumb at business events."

"How kind of her."

"Just don't, Faith." He set his jaw. "This is hard enough, all right?"

She shrugged.

"I literally drank just a couple of sips. But she made up for my part and got a bit tipsy." Lance squirmed. "After we'd finished our work, she wanted a tour of the house. I showed her our room, and—"

He swallowed again, drew his hand over his mouth, and rubbed his chin. "She started coming on to me."

Faith's heart pounded. *Oh, God! I can't hear this!*

Lance reached across and took Faith's hands in his. "I'm so sorry, Faith. We kissed. On the bed. But that was it. I told her we were violating office policy and had to stop. Since she was too drunk to drive home, I told her to sleep right there. I slept in the guest room, and she was gone in the morning when I woke up." He squeezed her hands tenderly. "I shouldn't have let it go that far, and I've had nothing to do with her since. She means nothing to me!"

Faith jerked her hands away and jumped off the love seat. Such lies! "Which is why you were making out with her at the airport today!"

Lance stood as well, his outrageously gorgeous eyebrows plunging as if he didn't understand her. Such a good actor!

"Making out? What are you talking about?"

"You butt dialed me, and I heard it all. You and Katrina at the airport—sharing a bit of intimacy. Disgusting! What kind of a creep are you?"

Lance's hands flew to his head, and he tugged on his spiked hair. "Would you slow down? You're making no sense!"

"Hand me your cellphone." Faith shoved her open palm toward him. "I'll prove it."

Slowly he pulled his cellphone from his back pocket and placed it in Faith's hand. She tapped a few times and pushed it back at him. "See this call at 1:33? You called me—but we didn't talk, did we? I heard you and Katrina carrying on with all kinds of background noise. That's when you were at the airport, right?"

Shaking his head, Lance stared at the screen. He returned the cellphone to his pocket, then slumped onto the love seat with his chin in his hands. "That's really weird. Let me think." After a moment, his eyes brightened. "Wait! My phone was missing—and I didn't know it. Katrina gave it back to me—told me I'd left it on the table at the restaurant where we all ate after we checked in for our flight. That was probably around 1:45 or so."

Faith shook her head. "Not bad—but remember I'm a fiction writer." She whirled on her heels and headed for the stairs. "I recognize fantasy a mile away."

Lance dogged her steps. "Wait, Faith! I can prove I slept in the guest room!"

In the upstairs hallway Faith spun around to face him. "How?"

"You know our wedding picture you put in my office a couple months ago?"

Faith drew her lips tight.

"I brought it up to the guest room and slept with it. I wanted *you* that night, not Katrina!"

He guided her toward the guest room, but she already knew what she'd see.

"Now that I think of it, I probably left my water glass in there, too." He swung the door open and strode to the nightstand. "Oh—maybe not. But here's the picture."

He picked it up and pulled her close.

His arm around her shoulder felt so good. Could it be true? Had he really chosen to sleep with their wedding photo rather than with the other woman? Or had he just happened to remember that Isme had left the picture in here—and was working it into his alibi? Attorneys were quick thinkers—

always ready to twist evidence their way.

"Now let me show you something." She wiggled out from his embrace. "Come with me."

In their bedroom, she pulled aside the decorative pillows from their bed and folded down the mauve comforter, exposing the blue pillowcase and sheets. With her hands on her hips, she stared at Lance, waiting for an explanation.

He looked from the bed to her face several times. "Am I missing something?"

Faith adopted her best school teacher pose. "You have fifteen seconds to tell me how those blue sheets got there and what happened to the mauve ones. If you can do that, I'll believe your story."

Lance raised his palms to the ceiling and shook his head as if utterly stymied. She had him.

His forehead wrinkled. "You put them on?"

She picked up the pillow and whacked it across his abdomen. "You lose; game over."

She turned to exit the room.

Lance's hand on her shoulder spun her around toward him, and his face contorted in anger. "I've tried to be honest with you, and you keep accusing me of stuff I know nothing about! You're gaslighting me! You could have made up what you heard on that phone call and changed the sheets yourself. You want to use my one mistake to end our marriage? So you can keep this house and drain me for every penny? Do you have a lover?"

Faith raised her hand to slap his face, but he

caught it and shoved it away.

She felt her face flame. "How dare you speak to me that way when you lay there with another woman on our bed?" She flung her hand toward the crime scene. "I've never looked at another guy since I met you—and you've been ogling women online and flirting with Katrina for months! I know both you and Katrina left the gala early. Am I supposed to believe that's a coincidence? If you sleep with her under our own roof, what's to keep you from sleeping with her in a hotel in another city? Even your own mother knows you've got adultery in your eyes!"

That struck home. Faith stayed long enough to see the pain on Lance's face, then ran to the guest room and locked the door. But she needn't have done so. He didn't follow.

# Chapter 8: Cat's Claw

So eleven years of marriage were ending just like that. Faith had heard Lance up early, getting ready for work, but she'd been too obstinate to face him. After he left, she checked the bedroom. His suitcase and all his personal hygiene items were gone. He left no note.

Could she have foiled things more expertly? She hadn't tried to hear from the Holy Spirit. She hadn't listened to Lance. She'd called him a creep and an adulterer and tried to slap him. Even if she found a way to forgive him, he might never forgive her. She had driven him back to Katrina's arms.

She went for a swim, showered, and made coffee. Finally she pulled out her Bible. She read the Beatitudes and then the love chapter. *Love bears all things and believes all things.* If so, she hadn't shown love toward Lance. Did he love her enough to bear with her anger and foolishness? Could they find a way to go on?

To do so, he'd have to own up to the phone call and the sheets. If he wanted her to believe his story—that he hadn't been unfaithful beyond a single moment of temptation—he'd have to honestly explain the remaining mysteries. He couldn't expect her to deny her own eyes and ears. And she wasn't about to cover up his wrongs.

Where was God now? Where was the new thing He was building from her failures? Women went on after divorce. She could go back to teaching. Was that what God wanted? Their affluence had allowed her to become too inner-focused. Teaching would force her to invest in others rather than keep wallowing in her own losses. She could help Gretchen with the grief support group—or maybe she'd need to find a divorce recovery group. She would have to depend on God. She'd have no one else. Even Isme would be hers only part time.

As she paced the silent house from one end to the other, she knew the time had come. She made her way to the storage room for some empty totes. With tears streaming down her cheeks, she packed up every nursery item in Blake's room. The blanket, the sheets, the mobile, the rug, the waste basket. She ran her hands over each piece and said goodbye to her dreams as she laid each one into its container. She stowed the totes back in the basement.

She fretted all the way to Jen's house to pick up Isme. Surely Jen would give up on her now—she hadn't followed any of her advice. She was hopeless. But Jen pulled her aside and prayed with her. Urging her not to despair, she begged her to call Lance. But Faith didn't know what she would say to him. It was up to him now—and God.

Late in the afternoon when she was running a load of laundry, she heard her phone vibrate. Lance had sent a text: *Katrina and I will be there at 6. Meet us poolside. Send Isme to Maddie's. Let's settle everything tonight.*

Her stomach churned. What was the point of meeting the other woman? Did Lance merely want to rub salt into her wounds? If he intended to leave her for someone else, she'd rather never see him again. Couldn't they handle all the divorce paperwork via email?

With her heart pounding, she arranged with Maddie's mom to keep Isme there until she got a text telling her to come home. She put on her prettiest sundress and highest-heeled sandals. She styled her hair and applied her make-up to perfection. If this was to be a showdown, she'd be fully equipped. She went out to sit under the poolside umbrella. Thankfully today was on the cool side—so Katrina wouldn't see her sweat.

From the corner of the pool enclosure, she heard, but couldn't see, two cars descend the driveway. The car doors slammed shut, and a feminine giggle wafted from the parking pad—the giggle she'd heard over the phone. Faith felt nausea rising, but she steeled herself.

Soon Katrina and Lance appeared. Both carried briefcases, and Lance lightly guided

Katrina by the elbow as she walked in stiletto heels down the pavers toward the pool. Katrina smiled up at Lance and chatted flirtatiously—though Faith couldn't catch any words. Even from this distance, Katrina was striking in a black dress and red jacket —setting off Lance's red shirt and charcoal suit. They could be a pair of movie stars emerging from a limo at the Oscars. Even with her own best clothing and make-up, Faith thought, she was out of their league.

When they entered through the pool gate, Katrina noticed Faith for the first time, and her face froze. Up close Katrina was gorgeous. Her ebony hair tumbled down her back in silky waves below her shoulder blades. Her perfectly arched dark eyebrows set off her stunning blue eyes, and her glistening full lips parted to show gleaming white teeth. And she was tall—nearly Lance's height—although three inches of that came from her shoes. A long string of red beads hanging across her chest accentuated her curves. With her skirt ending a couple of inches above her knees, she displayed plenty of shapely leg.

But seeing Faith had clearly thrown her off guard, which sparked Faith's courage. After all, Faith had the home field advantage, if nothing else.

Faith rose, summoning every ounce of poise and class, and crossed the pool deck to meet the obvious victor. She allowed her sandals to clack definitively across the textured concrete. Extending her hand, she flashed what she hoped was a gracious smile. "You must be Katrina."

Reluctantly the woman accepted Faith's hand and barely squeezed.

Lance dropped Katrina's elbow and stepped to Faith's side, draping his arms around her shoulders and planting a kiss on her cheek. "Thanks for meeting us, honey." He faced Katrina. "This is my wife, Faith. Let's sit down."

Stunned, with Lance's kiss still tingling, Faith lowered herself into the far chair. Lance was on her side? Confusion swirled in her brain, but an ember warmed her chest.

Katrina eyed the gate as if contemplating escape, but she took the seat Lance pointed to under the umbrella. Lance slipped off his suit coat, draped it over the back of his chair, and sat between the two women.

"Katrina, I know I said I wanted to go over some files. You'll forgive me for that little ruse." He reached over and grasped Faith's hand. "We're really here to put Faith's mind at ease. I want you to tell her what happened last Thursday night."

When the words registered in Faith's brain, an unsettling mix of hope and dread almost overwhelmed her. Perceiving Katrina's discomfort, she held her breath and studied Lance's face. What was he up to?

Her lips pursed, Katrina uncrossed and crossed her legs. She squared her shoulders. Again she eyed the gate, then turned back to Lance. "I see. Well, then. If you're sure that's what you want."

Faith recoiled at how harsh Katrina's voice had turned. How could such a lovely creature produce such a steely sound? She would hate to meet this woman in court.

Katrina fingered her necklace as she fixed her blue eyes on Faith. "Last Thursday I tried unsuccessfully to seduce your husband."

Lance kept a straight courtroom face, but Faith felt her mouth open and her eyes grow wide at the frank confession.

He gestured. "Go on. Provide as many details as you want—in your own words, of course."

As Faith forced herself to sit stoically still, Katrina told a story that matched Lance's, ending with Lance abandoning her in the bedroom and Katrina leaving before he awoke.

"Thank you." Lance checked Faith's reaction, then looked toward Katrina again. "Did I prime you in any way for the information you just gave?"

With a subtle snort, Katrina lifted her chin. "Hardly."

Lance motioned to Faith with an open palm. "The prosecution may now question the witness."

Faith bit her lip. Lance was playing this for all it was worth, while Katrina obviously found zero humor in the situation. If this wasn't so uncomfortable for Katrina, Faith might have been irritated by this little courtroom drama Lance had staged. But seeing Katrina's reaction, Faith had to appreciate Lance's strategy.

"Tell me," Faith asked coolly, "what color sheets were on my bed when you slept in it?"

Katrina answered without hesitation. "Light purple. Mauve."

Faith clenched her fists so hard that her nails bit her palms. "Then can you tell me why, when I returned from my trip on Friday afternoon, I found blue sheets on my bed?"

To Faith's surprise, Katrina leaned back in her chair and a wide grin spread across her face. "Perhaps."

Lance steepled his fingers in front of his chest.

Faith cleared her throat. "*Will* you tell me why, please?"

Eyeing Lance, Katrina subtly wiggled her head, causing her long locks to shimmer. She slowly steepled her fingers. "I may need to plead the fifth."

Tapping his foot, Lance looked between the two women. "Whatever you say will remain private. Your words will not be used to bring any action against you. Obviously, you have information you could use against me with our employer, and I have the same against you. We have good reason to keep each other's confidence. I'm sure Faith agrees."

Faith nodded.

"If there's one thing I despise," Katrina began, running her fingers through her hair and letting the locks arrange themselves onto her shoulders, "it's rejection." She reached into her handbag and pulled out a gold cigarette case. She removed a cigarette and held it between her fingers but made no attempt to light it. "I believed Lance was as interested in me as I was in him. He certainly encouraged me to think so. And once I got him on the bed, I knew he wanted me."

Faith's stomach flipped, and she started to rise from her chair, but Lance extended his arm to restrain her. "Let her continue."

"But just like that, it was over, and he left me by myself. Alone in another woman's bed. *That* was not a good feeling. When I feel put down, I take comfort in old habits." She waved the cigarette. "So I lit one up. But, as I said, I'd had a little too much to drink, and my coordination was ... lacking. I burned a hole in those pretty purple sheets." She tapped the cigarette into her palm. "In the morning when I came to my senses, I knew I had to replace the sheets. I'm not without conscience, you know. What kind of house guest leaves a cigarette burn in her host's sheet, after all?"

She snapped the cigarette back into the case and returned the case to her bag. "I showed my face at the office—you saw me, Lance, though you avoided me—but then I popped out. I searched for the sheets at several stores—but you have quite a unique color scheme, you know. Your mauve isn't easy to find. And time was running out. I knew Lance would be home to pack for the trip in another hour. So I grabbed any old set—you'd know they were different anyway. I let myself into the house—"

Lance leaned forward and glared at her. "What? How?"

Katrina laughed. "I have methods."

Lance gripped the arms of his chair with both hands, as if he could scarcely keep from lunging at the woman. "I want to know how you unlocked my door and disarmed my security system."

Faith shivered. She'd seldom seen Lance so riled.

Flashing ten long red nails, Katrina lifted her impeccably manicured hands into a surrender pose. "It was quite simple, really." She flung her hair over her shoulders with first one hand, then the other. "I found the key to the front door inside the garden gnome. That took me … oh, about thirty seconds. I'd seen you cancel the alarm when we got here the night before. Since I already knew Isme's birthday, I only had to verify the pattern you pressed."

Lance glowered at her.

She tossed her head, sending her hair rippling. "I'm very observant, and I have a keen memory for dates."

Faith could read Lance's mind when he glanced her way. They'd be changing their security code to something completely obscure. "So you put the blue sheets on the bed and disposed of the mauve ones."

"And while I was at it, I decided to leave my

calling card." Katrina raised one eyebrow coyly. "Did you find it?"

Faith tilted her chin. She wouldn't give her the satisfaction. "Calling card?"

"A hair on the pillow." She clicked her nails on the metal arm of her chair. "To remember me by," she purred.

Lance sneered with disgust. "Are you in therapy?"

Katrina's laugh rang out loudly as she stood to leave.

"Wait! One more question." Faith rose as well, motioning her to sit. Both women settled into their chairs again. "Did you call me from Lance's phone yesterday?"

Katrina smirked.

Lance growled, "You pick-pocketed my phone, didn't you?"

"Let's just say when I found it within my grasp—" she sensuously mimed caressing the phone by rubbing one long-fingered hand with the other— "I was momentarily tempted. You know how *that* feels, don't you, Lance?"

She aimed a long index finger at Lance and curled it slowly back toward herself.

Lance stood. "I've heard enough. You need help, Katrina, you really do."

Rising to face him, Katrina's face hardened. "Don't lecture me. You need to learn not to lead a woman on and then spurn her. You both got what you deserve." She slid the thin strap of her handbag over her shoulder with a sexy shrug. "Oh, and Lance? Don't worry about our working relationship being awkward from now on." She picked up her briefcase. "We won't have one. I submitted my resignation today. The Chicago firm made me a terrific offer—with better fringe benefits." Widening her eyes suggestively, she smiled and nodded first at Lance and then at Faith. "Don't trouble yourselves. I can show myself out. I've done it before."

She strode across the pool deck and exited through the gate. They watched her make her way back up the pavers and disappear around the front of the house. In a moment they heard her car roar up the driveway and down the street.

Lance lowered himself into his chair and dropped his head into his hands. His posture convinced Faith he was truly sorry for his behavior. Her heart throbbed with love for him— she was ready to forgive.

She sprang up and in a second wiggled her way onto his lap. He drew her into a long, luxurious kiss. When they parted, he held her face near, stroking her hair.

"Now do you believe she's nothing to me?" he whispered into her ear. He kissed her again, running his hands up and down her back. "I don't know why I ever thought she was attractive. I'm crazy about blondes—well, one blonde, that is."

One more kiss, and Faith was ready to head toward the bedroom, but she remembered their daughter. "I'd better text Isme."

"I'll do it." Lance pulled out his phone. "I miss that little girl like crazy!"

He completed the text, then reached for his briefcase. With Faith still on his lap, he pulled the chair she'd been sitting in close and hoisted the case onto it.

Faith drew his arm back around her waist. "Can't that wait?"

His expression grew serious, and he shook his head. "Absolutely not." He reached around her waist and clicked open the latches, then pulled out a package covered in iridescent wrapping paper with a flagrant, oversized bow. He placed it in her lap. "Go ahead. Open it."

She tore the wrapping off and laughed. In her hands she held a package of king-sized mauve sheets.

Lance kissed the back of her neck. "It took my assistant half the day to find these. You *do* have a unique color scheme."

She slid off his lap and pulled him to his feet. "C'mon. I need to get these in the wash so we can use them tonight."

She strolled seductively through the gate, then kicked off her sandals and dashed onto the lawn. He caught up with her, grabbed her around the waist, and twirled her in a dizzying circle. He set her down, and they walked hand in hand toward the side yard.

Faith nodded toward the new plantings.

"That's where I nearly put your mom's eye out. She told me I was a force to be reckoned with."

Lance laughed and squeezed her hand. "She got that right!"

"We should have your folks over soon— there's something they want to tell you."

Lance started to ask what, but she placed her finger over his lips—his luscious lips that were all hers now. "Why did you pack your suitcase this morning? I thought you weren't coming back."

"I was ready to give you space if you needed time to forgive me. I deserved some time in the dog house." He brushed his hand under her chin. "Will you forgive me? Can you?"

"With all my heart!" She planted a kiss on his lips. Still, this wouldn't be the end of it. She led him to the glider, and they sat together on the same side. She took his hand in hers. "Forgiving's not forgetting, you know."

Lowering his eyes, he nodded.

"Gretchen gave me the name of a marriage counselor—he's supposed to be terrific. I think we should schedule an appointment."

"Sure. Let's do that." He intertwined his fingers with hers. "And by the way, I talked with Tim today. He's already got me into a guy's accountability group."

He was a good man. They'd come out of this with a closer relationship than ever. She leaned her head against his arm. "How did you know she'd tell the truth? What if she lied and accused you of something you didn't do?"

Lance scoffed. "I'm a far better lawyer than she is. I'd have poked holes in her story in a millisecond—and she knew it. She's seen me in court."

Faith stroked his bicep. "Still, that was a gutsy thing to do."

He circled her shoulders with his arm. "I'm a gutsy guy." He played with her hair, curling it behind her ear. "No whistling past the graveyard for me."

They rocked in silence for a minute, and she snickered softly.

"What's funny?"

"They say seeing is believing, but sometimes understanding what we see is as hard as understanding what we don't see."

Lance chuckled. "That's a deep thought—"

"From a shallow mind!" they finished in unison.

"Mom! Dad! Come quick! Look!"

Isme's voice sounded from the front of the house. Faith shivered. The last several times Isme had called her to look at something, things hadn't turned out so well.

Lance grabbed the sheets, and they ran toward the parking pad where Isme met them with her finger to her lips. Motioning them to follow her, she tiptoed toward the front entry. As they rounded the corner of the garage and the front sidewalk came into view, they stopped.

Isme looked around in confusion. "Where did they go? They were here a minute ago!"

"What were?" Lance asked, following Isme's gaze.

Faith's heart sank. Another vision. She stroked Isme's sweaty back.

Isme pulled away. "The ducks! There was a whole family of ducks walking up the sidewalk like they owned the place. The daddy—he had a shiny green neck—the mommy—she had brown spots—and three fluffy yellow ducklings! They were so cute!"

Shaking his head, Lance squinted at Faith. "It's way past time for ducklings."

"And you couldn't have seen that, honey," Faith said. "Father ducks abandon their mates before the ducklings hatch."

Isme's lower lip stuck out and her chin quivered. "Why do I keep seeing impossible things?"

Lance's eyes grew wide. "This has happened before?"

Faith patted his arm. "Don't worry. It's just God's way of telling us He's watching out for us." She pulled them both to her, one on each side, curving her arms around their waists. "And this vision's easy to figure out."

They both turned their faces to hers, and she smiled back first at her wonderful husband and then at her precious daughter. "We're a happy family—soon to be a growing one."

Spreading her feet into a *V* and bending her knees, Faith waddled forward, leading them up the sidewalk. "Make way for ducklings!"

# About the Author

**Rebecca May Hope** delights in reading and writing the well-crafted phrase. While wordsmithing is its own reward, her weekly writers' group provides the impetus to keep writing and polishing—so she has something to share with her fellow authors. Rebecca couldn't imagine a life without teaching. Her middle school, high school, and college classes give her a chance to share her passion for words with a new crop of young people each year. When she feels the need to follow Wordsworth's advice ("Up, up, my friend, and quit your books!"), you'll find her playing with her grandbabies; walking her rambunctious ninety-pound Labradoodle on the nature trails near her home in Champlin, Minnesota; or pampering her softer-than-air Ragdoll cat.

Learn more about Rebecca and her writing at www.RebeccaMayHope.com.

# Also from Gabriel's Horn

## *Silken Strands*
*A Novel of the Historic Oneida Community*

### by Rebecca May Hope

For seventeen-year-old Millie Langston, one hundred husbands are ninety-nine too many. But since she lives at Oneida Community in 1877, when she marries, all the men of the commune will be her husbands, and she'll be just one of many wives to them. Perhaps because she's read so many novels, she dreams of romance with just one man —someone like the handsome Outsider she met on the train.

But that's not Millie's only dream. At the commune, she has the chance to work full time as a writer—something unheard of in the outside world. Unexpectedly, she becomes a rising star, thanks to her mentor, Tirzah Miller, editress of the

Community newspaper. Tirzah expects Millie to submit to marriage as all the other girls have, so she arranges for Millie to meet with their new leader, Theodore Noyes, for her initiation as a communal wife.

Now Millie must decide what she values most. How important is it to belong? Is it worth her freedom? Arranged marriages are bad enough, but Millie faces a string of unwanted husbands after Theodore, including the aging prophet, Father Noyes, and the sinister, eye-patched Judge Towner. How can she avoid the inevitable without being expelled from the only home she's ever known?

Look for more at www.gabrielshornpress.com. Learn about new releases and new authors. Join our mailing list there.

Made in the
USA
Columbia, SC